Gold & Silver Silver & Gold

TALES OF HIDDEN TREASURE

Collected and retold by

ALVIN SCHWARTZ

Pictures by David Christiana

Farrar Straus Giroux

New York

Gold & Silver Silver & Gold

TALES OF HIDDEN TREASURE

Grateful acknowledgment is made to the following for permission to reprint copyrighted material:

The Beale Cypher Association: The Beale ciphers in the story "Three Ciphers" and the notes to the story.

The California Folklore Society: "The Shiny Black Wall" adapted from "California Miners' Folklore: Above Ground," p. 41, by Wayland D. Hand, California Folklore Quarterly I, 1942.

Dodd, Mead & Company, Inc.: "12 Fathom NE" and "Forty-five Pinholes" adapted from True Tales of Buried Treasure, *pp. 167–69, 242–72, by Edward Rowe Snow. Copyright © 1950, 1960 by Edward Rowe Snow.*

William Morrow & Company, Inc.: "The Fresno Tree" adapted from On the Old West Coast, Being Further Reminiscences of a Ranger, *pp. 60–71, by Horace Bell, edited by Lanier Bartlett. Copyright © 1930 by William Morrow & Company, renewed 1958 by Lanier Bartlett.*

University of Texas Press: "The Ring and the Arrow" adapted from Coronado's Children, *pp. 298–99, 300–1, by J. Frank Dobie. Copyright © 1930 by the Southwest Press; copyright © 1958 by J. Frank Dobie; copyright © 1978 by the University of Texas Press.*

Viking Penguin, Inc.: "Under the Silk-Cotton Tree" based on "One Handful" from Whistle in the Graveyard *by Maria Leach. Copyright © 1974 by Maria Leach.*

For Ellie

CONTENTS

He dreamed that he had discovered an immense treasure in the center of his garden. At every stroke of the spade he laid bare a golden ingot; diamond crosses sparkled out of the dust; bags of money turned up their bellies fat with pieces of eight . . .

—Washington Irving, *Wolfert Webber, or Golden Dreams*

Gold & Silver Silver & Gold

TALES OF HIDDEN TREASURE

The Search

WHEN I WAS EIGHT OR NINE, there was a big empty lot near where I lived. It was filled with weeds and rocks, but it was the only open space in my neighborhood, and I spent a lot of time there.

One day on my way home from school, I turned over a rock to see if there were any worms under it. Instead, I found six old coins pressed into the soil—dimes, nickels, and pennies, all black and green with age. There must be more, I thought. I got a sharp stone and began digging and dug up another dime and another penny.

By then it was almost dark and I had to get home for supper. I could hardly wait to get back to that treasure hole. I dug there every day after school for a week, but there was nothing more. I took the money I had found and spent it on a movie.

Now and then, people do find a treasure by chance. There are such stories in this book. But often a treasure hunt is quite different than that. A person hears a tale of a lost mine or buried gold or a sunken pirate ship. And if it seems possible to find it, he may try his luck.

One of the most famous tales of treasure led thousands to search for riches beyond imagination. It is a story that goes back over five hundred years to the Chibcha Indians in South America.

Whenever the Chibchas chose a new chief, they followed an ancient ritual. They covered his naked body with powdered gold so that he glistened like a living statue. They took him from their village to the center of a deep lake where they believed a goddess lived. There he plunged into the icy water and washed off the gold.

Singing and shouting, his tribe threw jewels and objects of gold into the water as offerings to the goddess. For years, such riches drifted to the bottom of that treasure lake, where they lay waiting in the sand.

The story of the golden man spread far and wide. As one person told another, the story grew. People said the Chibcha chief dressed in powdered gold each morning and washed it off in the lake each evening. They said he lived in a golden city that glistened in the sun. They called him El Dorado, the golden one, and they gave his imaginary city the same name.

When explorers from Spain and elsewhere came to the New World in the sixteenth century, they were fascinated by the story of this golden city, El Dorado. Many of them spent years hunting for it in the mountains and the jungles. One explorer traveled the length of the Amazon River in his search. Another decided that the treasure lake was Lake Guavavita in the Andes Mountains and tried to drain the water from it. In their search they came upon many treasures, but they never found the golden city, for it existed only in their dreams.

Treasure hunters today still follow their dreams. They may spend years searching for a treasure, find nothing, and try elsewhere. Yet there always are some who eventually find what they are after. It may be a chest of gold coins, like the one Edward Rowe Snow uncovered with the help of a metal detector. Or it may be a treasure worth millions, like the one Mel Fisher found on the ocean floor after searching nineteen years for two Spanish galleons.

Everyone who hunts for treasure dreams of striking it rich. But often it is more than money that attracts them. It is the hunt itself. There is the mystery of just where treasure is. There is the adventure in tracking it down. And there is the excitement of digging into the ground, or blasting away sand on the ocean floor, or crawling deep into a cave, and finding it—if it is there.

ALVIN SCHWARTZ

1

A TREASURE FOUND

Not everyone who searches for treasure finds it. But the place to start in a book of treasure tales is with the story of two young men who did.

12 Fathom NE

ON A STORMY NIGHT IN THE YEAR 1880, an old man knocked on the door of a house in Middlesex, Vermont. He was carrying a small sea chest. A woman named Emaline Lewis came to see who it was.

"I don't know anybody in this town," he said. "But I have gotten a job in a logging camp near here. Could I leave my sea chest here until I come back?"

"Of course you can," she said. She put it away in the attic for him, but he never came back.

Mrs. Lewis had a young nephew named George Brenner, who lived in Boston. He was fascinated by the sea chest. Each time he visited his aunt, he asked her to open it, but each time she refused. "It's not my property," she would say.

After waiting twenty years, she decided that the man probably had died, and finally she and George opened the chest. No identification was inside, but there were some personal possessions—a whale's tooth, a quadrant, some seashells, and a letter from England dated 1830—and there was a very old map.

It was a map of the Kennebec River in Maine. A star had been drawn at a point alongside the river south of Augusta. Underneath the star, someone had written the following:

Stand abrest qurtsbolder bring in line with hill N ½ m
it lise 12 fathom N E near big trees under stone

George was certain that the star meant treasure. A few months later, he and a friend began to explore the shores

of the Kennebec in a small boat, looking for the quartz boulder mentioned on the map. They started near Boothbay Harbor, where the Kennebec empties into the Atlantic Ocean, and worked their way upstream.

Finally, they saw a huge boulder glistening in the sun and beached the boat. They sighted the boulder so that it lined up with a hill to the north. They walked northeast twelve fathoms, or seventy-two feet. And they looked for big trees, but could find only one. When it started to get dark, the two friends went back to Boothbay Harbor.

The next morning, they returned with shovels, a crowbar, and some canvas bags, in case there was any treasure to be carried away. They continued to search for other big trees and finally discovered the remains of a large stump. Now they were sure they were in the right place.

The directions said to look under a stone nearby, but there was no stone. Over the years, it must have been covered by soil, they decided. Probing the ground with the crowbar every few feet, they finally found a large flat stone.

They pried it up and pushed it over. Under the stone lay a smaller one. And under that stone was a small barrel covered with green mold, its top partly rotted away.

George reached inside and brought up a handful of gold coins. The barrel was filled with them! The two friends dipped their hands into the barrel again and again, letting the coins run through their fingers. There was also a roll of rotting canvas inside the barrel, but they did not bother to open it. The two of them felt as rich as the richest men on earth.

They filled the canvas bags, loaded them into their boat, then went all the way back to Boston, 150 miles away, without stopping. Two days later, they tied up at the North Avenue Public Landing. There, one guarded the sacks of money, while the other went to hire a horse and wagon.

They headed immediately for a bank, where experts examined the coins and opened the roll of canvas. Inside the canvas were a necklace of pearls and a cross nine inches high, studded with diamonds. The treasure was worth $20,000, which the bank gave the two young men that very day. Now that would be over $200,000.

2

A TREASURE LOST

There are thousands of places where someone found gold or silver, actually held it in his hands, even took some away with him. Then something happened. A map was lost. Directions were forgotten. A landslide occurred. And the place could not be found again. Even now, the treasure awaits.

Gold Lake

THE YEAR WAS 1849. The place was Downie's Flat, a gold-mining camp high in the Sierras, in northern California. It was still autumn, but snow was already falling.

On the night on which this story begins, the only light in Downie's Flat came from a tent that served as the local saloon. As usual, it was crowded with prospectors. Then a stranger staggered in, covered with snow and weak with exhaustion.

"My name is Robert Stoddard," he said, "and I come from Philadelphia." While traveling through the mountains, he told them, his wagon train had gotten lost. When they ran out of food, he and another man went hunting for a deer. But they could not find their way back. They wandered for days, then followed a river to a small lake.

"When we kneeled to drink, we saw nuggets of gold everywhere," he said. "The bottom of the lake and the shore were covered with them. We filled our pockets and a knapsack I was carrying. To find our way back, we tried to memorize the different peaks and the lay of the land. Then we followed a stream down the mountains."

The next day, Indians attacked them. The two ran off in separate directions. So that he could run faster, Stoddard threw away the knapsack. After that, he wandered in the mountains until he saw the light from the saloon.

That was his story. When he finished, he pulled out a handful of nuggets and threw them on the table.

The men in the saloon questioned him closely about Gold Lake, as they began to call it. Like many, they believed that there were fountainheads of gold high in the mountains that were the source of all the gold below. Maybe Gold Lake was such a place.

Stoddard wouldn't tell them any more. He was going to San Francisco, but he would be back.

True to his word, Stoddard returned the following spring, showing up at a mining camp farther down the mountain. He was looking for twenty-five men who would put up the money and join him in a search for Gold Lake. Such men were easy enough to find.

But soon the story of the expedition spread far and wide. When Stoddard and the twenty-five left on their search for Gold Lake, hundreds more, weighed down with equipment and supplies, followed them in a great parade. And hundreds of others were heading for the mountains to join them.

At first, the going was easy. But when the trails gave out, there were steep cliffs to scale and swollen streams to cross, and some of the treasure hunters were injured or killed. Meanwhile, the party followed its leader this way and that as he tried to recall the landmarks he had attempted to memorize the year before.

For three days, they were trapped in a gorge by heavy rains and raging streams they could not cross. Then somebody said what they had all been thinking. Either Stoddard was crazy or he was planning to sneak off to Gold Lake himself, now that they had helped him come this far.

They accused him of misleading them and appointed a prosecutor and a jury to try him. The jury gave him forty-eight hours to find Gold Lake, or they would hang him.

There are two versions of what occurred next. One is that they hung him. The other is that he fled during the night and was never seen again. Whatever happened, the prospectors began looking for gold in the streams that had trapped them—and they found it. The place became one of the richest gold fields in California.

What of Gold Lake? Was there really such a place, or was

Robert Stoddard crazy? Years later, prospectors still were looking for it. Many believed that after Stoddard filled his knapsack with gold a landslide filled the lake. The gold is still there, they said, waiting to be found.

The Orange Trees

IN A REMOTE JUNGLE CANYON deep in the mountains of western Mexico, there was once an enormously rich gold mine. This was three hundred years ago, maybe more. Near the mine were a great white hacienda, a small chapel where each day Mass was said, and a large grove of orange trees. Because of the trees, the mine was called El Naranjal—The Orangery. It was said that even the gold from the mine was the color of the oranges.

For unknown reasons, the owners of the gold mine fled. The white hacienda, the chapel, and the mine were abandoned. Later, the river that flowed through the canyon flooded, and the mine caved in and filled with debris. The jungle reclaimed the land, but in its midst the orange trees continued to grow.

The tale of El Naranjal was handed down over the years. Some said that the bells in the chapel could still be heard ringing in the distance. Others wondered if there ever was such a place, or if it existed only in the tales they had been told. Many prospectors searched for the mine, but no one ever found it, as far as was known.

In the 1880s, a writer named Wallace Gilpatrick met a prospector who said he had seen El Naranjal. "I stared at him in amazement," Gilpatrick recalled. This is the story the prospector told him.

"I had been looking for gold north of Durango and was returning to the city by horseback. About sundown the first day out, I came to a small Indian *rancho* and asked if I could sleep there. The owner was an old white-haired fellow who lived alone, and he seemed glad to have company. When we had supper, I got out a flask of whiskey, which we shared. The talk turned to old mines. He told me he knew where there was a very rich mine with a ruined hacienda.

"He said that fifty years before, when he was a young man, the government had sent soldiers to get recruits for the army. To escape them, he went over the mountains and down the far side. At the bottom of a canyon, he came to an abandoned hacienda with an old gold mine. He picked up a piece of rock on the ore dump and saw that it had chunks of pure gold in it.

"When he said that there were many ancient orange trees there, I knew he had seen El Naranjal. I asked if he would take me to this place, but he would not say. He became very cautious, so I dropped the subject.

"The next morning, I waited for him to say something about the mine, but he did not say a word. He had treated me very well, so as I was leaving, I gave him my flask of whiskey. He put it in an old rawhide chest. Then he showed me a piece of rock. I knew it was the one he had picked up at the mine. I held it to the light. There were nuggets of gold in that rock as big as the ends of my fingers.

"He took me by the arm and led me to the corral. Pointing to the mountains, he asked if I could see a big peak shaped like a cone. He said that the trail he had followed to the mine crossed at that point. Then he said that if I wanted to see the mine, he would go with me to that peak and start me on the right trail. He said there were bears and wildcats on the other side, so I would need to go well armed. I also would need provisions for a week or more.

"I did not have the money for a prospecting outfit, but I told him that someday I would return and look for the mine. He said I was the first he had ever told. I promised that I would come back.

"Ten years later, I had my chance. I had been prospecting

for some rich Americans a few days' ride from the Indian's *rancho*. I had twenty men working for me, but we found nothing. So I called it off and took the four best men and some mules and went to see my old friend. I wondered if he was still alive.

"When we reached the *rancho*, I was met by a middle-aged man. He said the old Indian, who was his brother, had died a few years before. We spent the night there. I talked about old mines of which I had heard, but he did not seem interested. At last I asked him if his brother had ever told him about El Naranjal. 'He was going to show me how to get there,' I said.

"He eyed me suspiciously. Then he went to the old rawhide chest and pulled out a small black flask. He asked if it was mine. I said it once had been mine, but I had given it to his brother. He said he would show me the old trail the next day.

"It was near sunset when we reached the peak shaped like a cone. He got off his mule and began searching for the trail that went down the far slope. He gave a satisfied grunt. Holding aside the tall grass, he pointed to what might once have been a footpath.

" 'Follow that for two or three days,' he told me, 'and you should see the hacienda.' With a look of dread, he said, 'Godspeed,' and disappeared into the darkness.

"We started as soon as it was light. Following a trail that has not been used for fifty years is next to impossible. At times we lost it and spent hours beating about in dense chaparral before we found it again.

"By sunset on the first day, the trail had taken us to a large ledge of rock, then it disappeared. There was nothing to do but camp there for the night. At daybreak we hunted for the trail again. Finally I discovered it doubling back on itself, snaking into the brush. I sent two men ahead with machetes to clear the way, and we followed, leading the animals.

"When night fell, we still were working our way down the mountain. On every side there was chaparral. I have been in lonely places, but never one like that. There was not a sign of life. Not even a bird sailed overhead, except now and then a vulture.

"After we had supper, one of my companions asked me to turn back. He said the vultures had been following us for two days, and he and the others were afraid we were going to die. I told him I was sure we would make it in one day more and to be ready for an early start. I rolled myself in my blankets and slept.

"When I awakened, it was not yet light. But before I opened my eyes, I knew I was alone. I called out, and no one answered. They had deserted me in the night. When daylight came, I found that they had taken most of the food and had left me with only one mule. I cursed them until I was exhausted. I swore I would not give up until I had seen the mine. If I failed, the vultures could have my carcass.

"Leading my mule, I started down the trail, cutting through the brush with a machete. I kept at it all day, not even stopping to eat. At sunset, I came to a wide ledge of red sandstone. The footpath had been worn deep in the soft rock. It looked like I was close to the end, and I decided to push on. I mounted my mule. From now on, I would depend on her.

"Soon it was so dark I could not see four feet ahead. The mule was nervous. Several times she stopped and stood stock still. I got off again and again to make sure I was still on the trail. I rode a little farther, maybe a hundred feet. The mule came to a standstill. She snorted and began to tremble.

"When I urged her forward, she bolted and tried to run back up the mountain. I turned her around and forced her ahead a few more steps. But she stopped again and would not move. I dismounted. With my hand still on her halter, I took a step forward. I was stepping into space! But I

managed to scramble back. There was nothing to do but wait for daylight. I lay down and tried to sleep.

"When I awoke, the sun was high. I found myself near the edge of a precipice. I crawled to the edge and peered down. It was a sheer drop of maybe four thousand feet. It looked like the end of the mountain had been sliced off in some great disaster. Instead of sloping out, it plunged inward.

"As I gazed down into the jungle, my eye caught a shining thread of silver. It was a river, of course. Beside it was a large clump of bright green leaves—the orange trees. Through the leaves I could see patches of white—the walls of the hacienda.

"It was El Naranjal.

"Yet there was no way I could reach it. There was no way to get down—no trail, no rope, nothing. My mule was ready to drop. My food was gone. Unless I turned back, I would starve.

"I sat for hours, gazing at that clump of bright green and those patches of white. I was sure I could see the outlines of the buildings. Once I thought I heard bells chiming in the old chapel. I took a last look and started back up the mountain, dragging my mule after me."

The prospector made his way back to civilization, but he never made it back to El Naranjal. He had no money of his own, and there was no one who believed in his story enough to help him return.

A Shiny Black Wall

IN THE YEAR 1900 or thereabouts, a man on horseback rode into Johannesburg, California. He had been prospecting for gold in the desert to the east. Tied to his horse was a train of six burros. Each was carrying saddlebags filled with samples of ore.

He rode directly to the government assay office to learn if the ore contained gold. If it did, he would register a claim and start mining. The man gave the assayer an address in Los Angeles where he could send his report.

"Oh, I almost forgot," he said. "Take a look at these, too." He handed him a few pieces of shiny black quartz with white stripes running through them. "There's a whole wall of it out there," he said. "If it's worth anything, we'll go partners." He laughed and rode off. The assayer glanced at the rocks. He had seen too much black quartz to get excited.

Later, the assayer threw the rocks into the garbage burner, along with some chicken bones and other waste. He set it all on fire. When his wife took another load of garbage out to the burner the next day, her eyes almost popped from her head. The chicken bones were covered with gold.

"Come quick!" she shouted. When her husband saw the bones, he knew at once what had happened. The white stripes in the quartz were tellurium, a mineral that sometimes contains gold. When the fire heated the chicken bones, the lime in the bones had separated the gold from the rocks. If the prospector had found a whole wall of tellurium, he had struck it *very* rich.

The assayer went to Los Angeles to give him the good news. A woman in black came to the door. "Yes, I am his wife," she said softly, "or I was. He was killed by a streetcar a few days ago." But he had told her nothing of the shiny black wall. The secret of where it was had died with him. The assayer searched for that wall for six months and found nothing. Others are still looking.

3

PIRATE SHIPS AND SPANISH GALLEONS

The sunken ships that treasure hunters seek are fabulous treasure houses. When they sank in a storm or a battle, they were carrying fortunes in gold, silver, jewels, and other riches. Some were pirate ships, but there also were Spanish galleons, merchant ships, ocean liners, even warships. Thousands of such vessels wait on the ocean floor.

The Whydah

SAM BELLAMY WAS A FAMOUS PIRATE. But before he became a pirate, he'd had other plans. When he was a young man, in the west of England, he wanted to hunt treasure, not steal it.

Bellamy heard of a Spanish galleon loaded with silver coins that had sunk in the West Indies. In 1715, he sailed west in a tiny sloop to find that treasure. He stopped at Eastham on Cape Cod to rest and obtain supplies.

For several weeks he stayed at Higgins Tavern. One spring evening, according to legend, he went out for a walk. He heard someone singing under an apple tree near the burying ground and went to see who it was. There he met Maria Hallett, who was only fifteen and the prettiest girl in Eastham.

And they fell in love. Bellamy promised to come back and marry her when he found his treasure, and take her to the West Indies to live. Then he sailed away.

Maria gave birth to a child, but it became ill and died. She was "warned out" of Eastham, told never to come back. She went to live in the next town in a hut in a meadow overlooking the ocean and earned her living as a weaver. Meanwhile she waited for Sam Bellamy to return.

In the West Indies, Bellamy found the wreck he was looking for, but found no treasure. He'd spent all his money in the search and had nothing to show for it. This was no way to get rich. Frustrated and impatient, he turned pirate.

Bellamy and a friend used his sloop in raids on other vessels. They then joined with two other pirates who had their own ships, and Bellamy took charge. He and his men captured a big, clumsy craft called the *Sultana*, which he took for his own. But he yearned for a taller, faster, more graceful ship, which he could use to sail back to Maria Hallett in Eastham.

It turned out to be the *Whydah*, a vessel so lovely seamen called her the "paradise bird." Bellamy captured her in 1717, a year after she had been built to carry slaves from Ouidah in West Africa, for which she was named, to the West Indies. She was bound for Africa when Bellamy saw her and gave chase. He pursued her for three days and nights before he caught her.

Bellamy gave her captain the *Sultana* in exchange, then sailed north for Eastham. Between the *Whydah*'s decks he stored four hundred bags of gold and silver coins, uncounted bars of gold and silver, chests filled with pieces of eight, and other booty from the fifty vessels he had plundered.

The night they approached Eastham harbor, they were caught in a dreadful storm that threatened to drive them onto the shoals. With breakers just ahead, the crew cut down the mainsail with their cutlasses. Then Bellamy faced the *Whydah* into the storm and tried to sail away from the coast.

For hours the ship struggled against the wind but made no progress. Slowly she was driven back toward the breakers. A quarter of a mile offshore, the *Whydah* capsized in mountainous seas. Her decks fell out, then her innards, and her treasure spilled into the raging waters.

A hundred and one pirates drowned including Sam Bellamy. For days their bodies washed up on shore. Wreckage littered the beach for miles. For a while, what was left of the *Whydah* could be seen at low tide, but finally the wreck disappeared into the sand and silt.

What of Bellamy's love, Maria Hallett? As the story goes, a young girl who wanted a pattern for weaving went to her hut overlooking the ocean. Finding no one at home, she looked along the beach and there she found Maria's body. Maria had cut her throat.

And what of the treasure? Some said that the wreck was picked clean by local people, who kept what they found secret. But over the years, none of the treasure turned up. Many wondered if it ever had been found or if it even existed.

In 1984, a former high school teacher named Barry Clifford, from the nearby island of Martha's Vineyard, began looking for the *Whydah* and its treasure. Thirty-five people were backing him with their money. That year, he found an old ship off Marconi Beach in South Wellfleet. But he could not tell if it was the *Whydah* or some other vessel.

Using powerful blasts from the ship's propeller, Clifford and his crew dug two test pits in the sand on the ocean floor, each about eight feet wide and eight feet long.

In them they found a flintlock pistol, a broadsword, seven cannons, and a bronze ship's bell. On the bell were the words THE WHYDAH GALLY, 1716. They also found 180 bags of silver coins and gold dust, and that was only the beginning.

The Atocha

ONCE OR TWICE A YEAR a fleet of high-bodied, three-masted wooden galleons transported tons of gold, silver, and other riches from the Spanish colonies in the New World to Spain. The galleons carried not only treasure but also soldiers and cannons to protect it. These were the largest ships afloat in the sixteenth and seventeenth centuries, yet they were only a hundred feet long and weighed but six hundred tons.

One such treasure fleet sailed from Havana, Cuba, on Sunday, September 4, 1622. It consisted of eight galleons and twenty merchant ships. As usual, the galleons were badly overloaded, but their hulls were filled with ballast stones to give them stability.

The flagship of the fleet, *Nuestra Señora de Atocha*, carried a crew of one hundred and fifteen. There also were a hundred soldiers on board and forty-eight passengers, most of them rich businessmen, government officials, or priests. In the hold were forty-seven tons of gold and silver, as well as copper and tobacco.

Because of many delays, the fleet left for Spain during the hurricane season. It was something the Spanish rarely did. But the plan was to follow the usual route—north for ninety miles until they reached the Florida Keys, east with the Gulf Stream to Cape Canaveral, then across the Atlantic to Spain.

As the fleet approached the Florida Keys on the morning of September 5, a powerful hurricane screamed out of the northeast. It forced the ships apart, tore off their masts and rigging, and ripped out their rudders. When the wind shifted to the south, it drove several of them onto the reefs that guard the Keys.

The *Atocha* struck a reef ten miles southwest of the Marquesas Atolls, forty miles west of what today is called Key West. It sank immediately in fifty-four feet of water. Three miles away, the galleon *Santa Margarita* hit another reef. It sank in twenty-five feet of water as powerful waves tore it apart. Six other ships went down.

The loss of these ships and the great treasure they carried was a disaster for Spain. A team of pearl divers was quickly brought from Mexico to find the wrecks and salvage what they could. They had managed to bring up two of the *Atocha*'s bronze cannons, when another hurricane struck. It scattered the ship's wreckage so widely nothing more could be found.

Since the *Santa Margarita* had gone down in water only half as deep, salvaging her cargo was easier, but it took years. Eventually, divers brought up over two thousand tons of silver, but they could not find any of the gold that had been

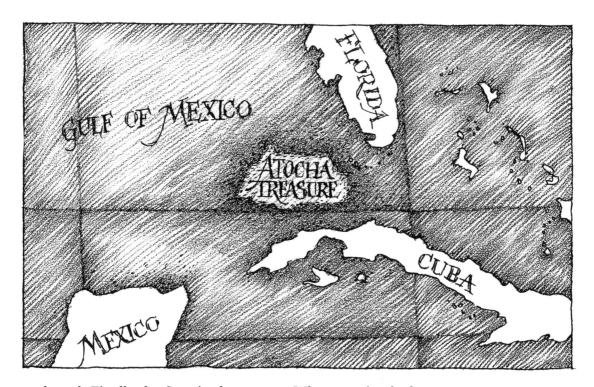

on board. Finally the Spaniards gave up. What remained of the two ships and the great wealth they had carried was gradually forgotten. The only record of what had happened was filed away in a musty archive in Spain. Soon it, too, was forgotten.

Three hundred and forty-four years later, in 1966, the search for the two vessels began again. This time, the treasure hunter was a former chicken farmer and divers' shop operator named Mel Fisher. Fisher had moved from California to Florida in 1962 to hunt for sunken treasure ships. With him were his wife and his three young sons, Dirk, Kim, and Kane.

With friends, Fisher soon found the remains of a treasure galleon in the Atlantic Ocean off Fort Pierce. A curator at the Smithsonian Institution, in Washington, D.C., then told him about the *Atocha* and the *Santa Margarita*, and he decided to search for them.

Here is a record of what happened:

1966. From what was then known of the *Atocha*, Fisher believed that it had sunk off the Matecumbe Keys, east of Key West. It was there that he planned to search. As we now know, the ship actually sank many miles to the west. Everyone assumed that the *Santa Margarita* was near the *Atocha*.

With two pieces of equipment he had used earlier, Fisher was sure he would find one ship or the other in just a week or two.

Part of this equipment was a magnetometer. As it was towed by a search vessel, the device recorded deposits of iron it passed over. Since most old ships contained some iron, it was a clue to where one might have sunk.

The other equipment Fisher had invented. It was a hood made of sheet metal that was fitted around the propellers of a search vessel. When the propellers rotated, their backwash was forced downward under great pressure. In minutes, it dug a hole twenty to thirty feet wide and ten feet deep, uncovering anything that was buried there. Fisher called his invention a "mailbox," because of its shape. (Such equipment also was used years later in the search for the *Whydah*, described in the previous story.)

In hunting for the two galleons, Fisher's crew towed a magnetometer back and forth across the open seas in straight lines no more than twenty feet apart, moving systematically from one section to another. They traveled over a hundred thousand miles in this part of their search.

Each time the "mag" registered a strong "hit," a diver went down to see what had caused it. If it seemed to be a buried object, they turned on a mailbox to remove the overburden of sand.

They found a baby carriage, a sunken freighter, an old airplane, and a torpedo from World War II, but not the *Atocha* or the *Santa Margarita*. The week or two Fisher thought the search would take stretched into four years.

1970. A friend of Fisher's, a scholar named Eugene Lyon,

was doing research on the history of Florida at a famous archive in Spain. In going through old records, he came across a report from 1622 that described how the Spanish tried to salvage the *Santa Margarita*.

The report confused him. It said that the *Santa Margarita* had sunk off the "Keys of Matecumbe." Then it said that it had sunk off the "Keys of Marquis," which today are known as the Marquesas Atolls.

Lyon remembered that the Spaniards had called *all* of the Florida Keys the "Keys of Matecumbe." It was clear that the *Santa Margarita*, and probably the *Atocha*, had been wrecked off the Marquesas Atolls, not off the two keys to the east that still are called Matecumbe. Fisher had been searching in the wrong place for four years.

Lyon quickly got in touch with Fisher, who moved to a new location a hundred miles to the west. But over the next eighteen months he still found nothing.

1972. South of the Marquesas Atolls, Fisher found a reef that extended east and west for ten miles. It seemed to him the kind of place where the two vessels might have met disaster. But there was no trace of them.

A few weeks later, the mag registered a strong hit five miles to the northwest. As a diver swam nearby, a mailbox dug out a huge anchor of the type Spanish galleons had used. A photographer who had gone with the diver saw a gleaming object fly by in the prop wash and caught it with his hand. It was a solid-gold chain, several feet long. And there was much more—muskets, swords, two bars of gold, and pieces of eight dated 1622, the year the two ships sank.

They were the first finds Fisher had made since he began his search six years before. But he did not know whether they were from the *Atocha*, the *Santa Margarita*, or some other old ship.

Using the anchor as a starting point, his search boats moved out in an ever-growing circle. Divers found pottery, hoops from barrels that had rotted away, cannonballs, and ballast stones. The ballast stones were of the most importance. When treasure hunters find the main pile of ballast from an old ship, often they find most of the treasure. But for the rest of the year, Fisher came up with nothing more.

Fisher asked Eugene Lyon in Spain to find out how large the *Atocha* and the *Santa Margarita* were, what they were carrying, and anything else that would help identify them. It meant going through thousands of documents written by hand. Lyon set aside his own research and went to work. Meanwhile, Fisher continued his treasure hunt.

1973. Fisher decided they needed more powerful mailboxes, which would dig deeper, wider holes. For these he needed boats with more powerful engines. He bought two old tugboats. He called one the *Northwind* and made his eighteen-year-old son, Dirk, its captain. He called the other *Southwind* and named his sixteen-year-old son, Kim, its captain.

On July 4, a blast from one of the new mailboxes uncovered three heavy black objects that looked like loaves of bread. When the black coating was scraped off, they turned out to be ingots of silver, each with its own serial number stamped on it—*569, 794, 4584.*

Then Eugene Lyon discovered a list of the cargo aboard the two galleons. It was two thousand pages long and included the number stamped on each ingot of silver and each bar of gold the ships carried. The ingots they had found were from the *Atocha*. It was the first proof they had that they were on the right track. But once again the trail went cold.

Fisher decided he needed more expert help if he was going to locate the rest of the wreck. He hired a marine archaeologist, who began to map where each of the finds had been made and record how they were connected. It soon became clear that the *Atocha*'s remains had been scattered over a wide area.

By studying the pattern, the archaeologist hoped to find

a trail of wreckage that would lead back to where the ship had gone down. There they would find the main ballast pile and the hold where most of the *Atocha*'s treasure had been stored.

1975. Dirk Fisher had moved the *Northwind* from where they had been searching to another location. One Sunday morning, swimming alone underwater in this new area, he saw on the ocean floor five bronze cannons in a heap, then four others scattered about, each with its own serial number. Lyon's list showed that they had been aboard the *Atocha*. Everyone was sure that the main hold and its treasure were nearby.

Just a week later, while its crew slept, the *Northwind* capsized and sank. The hose that carried sea water to the toilet broke. But the pump that drew the water into the ship continued to operate and filled the hull. Dirk, his wife, and a diver drowned.

Hunting treasure was Fisher's work. Despite his great grief, he continued the search. Again they lost the trail, and for over three years they found nothing.

1979. In a period of just two weeks, Fisher's divers brought up a gold chain that weighed ten and a half pounds, four bars of gold, a gold disk, and the stern anchor of the *Atocha*. But there was nothing more.

1980. Fisher was concerned that while he concentrated on the *Atocha*, others would beat him to the *Santa Margarita*. Unknown vessels had been prowling in the waters nearby. One of them had deliberately headed on a collision course with one of Fisher's search boats, then at the last minute swerved away. A second had fired five pistol shots across the bow of another of his boats.

Toward the end of the year, Fisher picked up a new trail about three miles east of where he had been searching. He now had a small magnetometer a diver could carry with him, which identified not only iron but other metals. It led them to a large copper kettle and an anchor. Working their way

north, they found coins, gold bars, and, most important, ballast stones.

1981. In April, they found more gold. In May, they uncovered more artifacts, including a large silver bell. A few days later, Kane Fisher, who was now twenty-one, saw on the ocean floor a half-dozen ingots of silver, and then—the whole stern end of the *Santa Margarita*, with its ribs and planks still in place! It was twenty-three feet long and sixteen feet across.

Near the stern, divers found a great clump of silver coins stuck together, still in the shape of the wooden chest that once had held them, then had rotted away.

All through the spring, summer, and fall, they brought up more and more of the *Santa Margarita*'s treasure: 118 pounds of gold, 180 feet of gold chain, 56 gold coins, 15,000 silver coins, and 18 ingots of silver. Together they were worth between $20 million and $40 million.

The stern was left where Kane had found it. It was the oldest and largest remnant of a Spanish galleon ever discovered in North America. Fisher decided not to raise it until it had been studied, mapped, and photographed.

1985. On July 20, Kim and Kane Fisher cleared away five feet of silt on the ocean bottom, using high-pressure hoses with water pumped from one of the search vessels. Underneath lay a great jumble of silver bars—a "silver reef," one of them called it. Next to this "reef," gold and silver coins spilled from a treasure chest. They finally had found the main hold of the *Atocha*.

One of the divers raced back to the search vessel with the news. "It's here!" he shouted as he broke the surface. "We found it! We found it!"

It was ten years to the day since Dirk Fisher had drowned and nineteen years since Mel Fisher had begun his search.

At last it was clear what had happened when the *Atocha* sank in one storm, then was torn apart by another. The second storm had scattered the galleon's remains over a distance of six miles. Plotted on an archaeologist's map, it looked like a giant cone, its point where the ship had gone down.

Starting with the huge anchor they had found in 1972, Fisher's crew had spent thirteen years following a trail of artifacts. Back and forth across the ocean floor they went, until they finally reached the point of the cone—and the treasure.

It was not far from the reef where, years before, Fisher thought the ship might have been wrecked. But at that time they had found nothing.

The value of the *Atocha*'s treasure was expected to reach almost four hundred million dollars. But Fisher said he would not sell his share. He would keep it together so that it could be seen and studied. He planned to exhibit it at various places so that, as he said, people could be "thrilled by holding the gold in their hands."

Each of the divers was to receive a share of the treasure worth over a hundred thousand dollars. Those who had been diving since the beginning of the search would receive a million dollars or more.

The night after the treasure was found, the crew had a big party in Key West. Together they sang "The Impossible Dream." Then they sang an old song called "We're in the Money."

4

THE PIT AND THE CAVE

The tales of treasure told in this chapter have been told in many places. Yet the treasures still wait to be found.

The Bank on Oak Island

ON A SMALL ISLAND off the southeast coast of Nova Scotia, not far from the town of Chester, there is a deep pit where there may be a vast treasure. People believe it might be a Viking treasure, or a treasure buried after a Spanish galleon lost its way, or a treasure left by pirates.

Of course, there may be no treasure at all. Yet that does not seem likely, after the trouble somebody took to dig that pit, then make sure that nobody could reach the bottom.

The pit was discovered in 1795, when three farmboys crossed over from the mainland. They wandered into a clearing where there was a giant oak tree. Strange figures had been carved in its trunk, and the end of a lower branch had been sawed off. The stump of the branch looked like a giant finger pointing at something.

What it pointed at was a big round depression in the ground. The depression looked like an old well that had been filled in. But from what the boys knew, no one had ever lived on the island. They went home and got some shovels and began digging.

A few feet down, they found a covering of flat stones. Under the stones was a shaft with walls of hard-packed dirt, but the shaft had been filled in with soil.

At ten feet, they came to the rotted remains of a platform made from oak planks. At twenty feet and again at thirty feet, they found the same thing. To go any deeper, they needed help, but they had no money to hire anyone, so they gave up.

A few years later, a doctor from a nearby town formed a

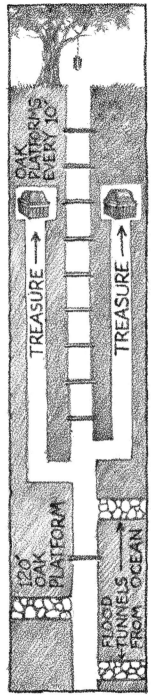

company to dig out the rest of the shaft. About every ten feet, they found the remains of still another platform. Then at ninety-five feet, they found a platform that had not rotted and that blocked their way. Since it was a Saturday afternoon, they decided to stop digging and continue the following Monday.

When they returned, they found much of the shaft flooded with water. Unable to bail all of it out, they bypassed the water by digging a new shaft next to the old one. They went down 110 feet, then dug a tunnel to the main shaft. When water burst in from above, they gave up.

In the 1850s, another team of treasure hunters tried to reach the bottom of the pit. They used a drill with a bit that brought up samples of whatever it moved through. Since the main shaft was flooded again, they lowered the drill through the water until it reached the soil below. Then they began drilling.

At ninety-eight feet, the drill went through a piece of oak four inches thick. Next it passed through twenty-two inches of what seemed to be pieces of metal—maybe coins, they thought. Then it penetrated another piece of wood. The two pieces of wood appeared to be a chest of some kind. The drill went through another "chest" like the first, and hit clay.

The bit on the drill brought up three small gold links and some coconut matting, a fabric that once was used in packing a ship's cargo. But since water blocked the way, reaching the bottom of the pit seemed impossible.

The following year, they sank a new shaft, just as treasure hunters had done fifty years before. But again water burst in from above. When they tried to pump it out, they discovered that it was salt water from the ocean. Of course, if the water flowed in through some natural channel, the main shaft could not have been dug in the first place. They decided that someone had arranged things so that the water would come in only at certain times.

They soon found where it was coming from. A system of drains on the shore five hundred feet away drew the water in at high tide. Every twelve hours, as the tide rose, it flowed into a tunnel, which flooded the lower part of the shaft. They tried to block the tunnel, but they could not stop the water.

In the years that followed, dozens of treasure hunters tried to dig out whatever was hidden in the pit. In 1909, a future President of the United States, Franklin D. Roosevelt, helped to organize a search. In the 1930s, someone brought in a steam shovel to dig out the shaft. In the 1950s, someone else brought in an oil-drilling rig. They found a small piece of parchment and an ivory boatswain's whistle. They also discovered two more flood tunnels. But that was all.

By then, the area had been dug up so often and was so muddy, a treasure could have shifted in any direction.

The most ambitious search began in 1965. These latest treasure hunters thought that the shaft was a kind of bank a group of pirates had used to hide their booty.

After the main shaft had been dug, they believed, each pirate dug his own secret tunnel out from the shaft, then up toward the surface, and stored his treasure there. The drawing shows how this might have been done.

The flood drains and tunnels were then installed to keep others out. As the last step, the shaft was filled in. When a pirate wanted his loot, he would pace off the distance from the top of the shaft to the area of his tunnel and dig there. That was their theory.

Over the next ten years, these treasure hunters worked in the main shaft and also sunk two hundred other shafts. Three men were killed in accidents and over a half-million dollars was spent. But whatever the pit held was not recovered. When this was written, the mystery still had not been solved.

Love, Death, and Gold

IN THE 1700S Miguel Peralta de Córdoba was the Baron of Colorado. In those days, Spain claimed all of what is now the American Southwest, and Peralta was in charge of what became the states of Colorado and Arizona.

The baron had a daughter, who fell in love with a man named Carlos. She saw him secretly until the dreadful day her brothers, Manuel, Ramón, and Pedro, discovered them together. When they drew their guns, he fled into the Superstition Mountains of Arizona, and they pursued him.

Whether they ever found Carlos is not known. But in trying to track him down, they did find a rich deposit of gold, which the family mined for over a hundred years.

One day in 1866, two of Peralta's great-grandsons, Enrico and Miguel, were at the family mine with their men, when they were attacked by Apache Indians. The Apaches claimed the mine was theirs, and they massacred everyone except the two Peraltas, who managed to escape.

Five years later, on a hot, dusty afternoon, two Germans, Jacob Weiser and Jacob Waltz, were watching a card game in a tavern in Arispe, Mexico. It soon became clear that one of the players was being cheated. When the man complained, another player stabbed him with a knife. Weiser knocked down the attacker and helped the wounded man to safety.

The man Weiser saved was Miguel Peralta. In gratitude, he told the Germans about his family's gold mine. But he said he was afraid the Apaches would kill him if he went back and tried to work it. "Protect me," he said, "and I will share the gold with you."

The two Germans did what he asked, then used their share of the gold to buy the mine from him. They began working it almost at once. Then Weiser was mysteriously killed. Some said Apaches had done it. Others said it was Jacob Waltz, who wanted the mine for himself. But nothing was ever proved.

Waltz worked the mine for many years, returning to it whenever he needed money. Of course, he kept the location a secret, and although many tried to follow him, no one ever succeeded. But just before he died, he told some friends how to find it.

He told them to start from a certain cow house they knew, then work their way over a mountain until they reached a big spring. There they would see in the rock an opening shaped like a funnel. In the hillside below the funnel was a cave which led to the mine.

There was another clue. An old Mexican woman said that when she was young she had gone to the mine with her sweetheart, who worked for the Peraltas. She had seen a row of three mountain peaks nearby.

A doctor named Abraham Thorne also had information. Once, he had been captured by the Apaches. When they learned he was a surgeon, they kept him prisoner for several years to care for members of the tribe who had been wounded in battle.

Before the Apaches released Thorne, they blindfolded him and took him to a canyon. When they took the blindfold off, the place he saw glittered with gold. They told him to fill his pockets with as much as he could carry.

Thorne said that he saw a ruined hut in the canyon and, in the distance, a formation of rock shaped like a Mexican hat. That rock formation is known today as Sombrero Butte and also as Weaver's Needle. Several others who claimed to have seen the mine said it was but a mile or so from Weaver's Needle.

Waltz's friends never found the mine, nor has anyone else. Yet, each year, hundreds of people search for the "Lost

Dutchman," as they call it in memory of the two dead Germans. If you find yourself in Phoenix, Arizona, the Superstitions are just to the east, near Mesa. You might try your luck.

5

THERE IT IS!

Most people who find treasure do so by chance. Often it is not of great value, but just *finding* it is exciting. A person is digging in a garden or walking on a beach—and there it is! That is what happened in Bayard, Iowa, one sunny afternoon after school. But it was only the beginning of the story.

Five Fruit Jars

ALL TWELVE MEMBERS OF A BOYS' CLUB called the Space Cadets were there. They were going to build a clubhouse on a vacant lot near the railroad tracks.

Marty Nissen moved an old drain tile and found a hole underneath. When he reached into the hole, he pulled out a rusty coffee can. Inside the can was an old fruit jar, and inside the jar were gold coins.

"Buried treasure!" he screamed. "We found buried treasure!"

Somebody else reached into the hole, and he pulled up another fruit jar filled with coins, then a third. By then, the boys were tackling one another in their excitement.

Altogether they pulled up five jars of gold coins and a package of old ten- and twenty-dollar bills. The more they found, the easier it was to imagine the cars, bikes, and other things they soon could buy for themselves. But it did not happen quite that way.

First the treasure had to be turned over to the sheriff, in case it belonged to somebody else. That was when things got complicated. The sheriff found that a house once stood where the boys had discovered the money. An old woman named Emma Beardsley had lived there, until she wandered out onto the railroad tracks one day and a freight train hit her. Had *she* hidden the money? Or was it some person nobody knew about? It was a question the sheriff could not answer.

The coins and bills the boys had found were worth $11,585. It was old-fashioned money that had not been in use for years. The coins were twenty-dollar gold pieces. The bills were so large, people used to call them "horse blankets."

The sheriff put the money in a bank in town. Under the law, it had to remain there for a year, to give people a chance to claim it. If no one did, the boys would get it back.

Just before the year was up, two people said the treasure was theirs. One was John Rosenbeck, the man who owned the lot where the boys had found the money. Since it was his land, he said the money should be given to him. The other was Mrs. Beardsley's niece, Mrs. Clyde Tallman. Since she was Mrs. Beardsley's only living relative, she said it should go to her. Now a judge would have to decide.

Another year went by. Finally a judge decided that the boys would get forty percent of the treasure and that Mr. Rosenbeck and Mrs. Tallman would each get thirty percent.

Just when everyone thought the problem was solved, the American Red Cross claimed the treasure. It turned out that Mrs. Beardsley had inherited money from her brother when he died. According to his will, the Red Cross was to get what was left when she died.

Many more months went by. The Red Cross suddenly dropped its claim, with no explanation. But all the boys cared about was that at last they were going to get their money.

The judge decided to have the coins and bills sold at auction. They were so old, collectors would buy them for more than their face value, and that would increase the size of the treasure. With the extra money, the treasure grew to almost $16,000.

A few weeks before Christmas, the boys finally got their share of the booty, after court fees, auction fees and other expenses were paid. As TV cameras filmed the scene, the mayor gave each of them a check for $478.36. Then they went out for ice cream. It was three and a half years since Marty Nissen had reached into a hole in the ground and pulled out a jar filled with gold coins.

6

CODES, MAPS, AND SIGNS

In a desolate area of scrub and brush on the coast of South Carolina, a man found a dead beetle with scales the color of gold. Nearby he found a piece of old parchment. On it was a drawing of a death's-head, a human skull.

When the man heated the parchment, the heat revealed the following cryptogram which had been written in invisible ink:

53‡‡†305))6*;4826)4‡.)4‡);806*;48†8¶60))85;1‡(;:‡*8†83
(88)5*†;46(;88*96*?;8)*‡(;485);5*†2:*‡(;4956*2(5*—4)8
¶8*;4069285);)6†8)4‡‡;1(‡9;48081;8:8‡1;48†85;4)485†
528806*81(‡9;48;(88;4(‡?34;48)4‡;161;:188;‡?;

The heat also disclosed a drawing of a young goat, or kid. The man decided that the cryptogram contained the directions to the famous treasure of Captain Kidd. It looked complicated, but he solved it.

First he counted the frequency of the numbers and symbols. The number *8* was used most often, which told him it stood for *e*, the letter that is used most often in English, which was Kidd's language.

Next he tried to find the characters that stood for *the*, the word that is used most often in English. He searched for a group of three characters that ended with *8*, or *e*, and that appeared again and again.

He quickly saw that *;48* stood for *the*. He also had identified two more letters. The semicolon stood for *t*, and the number *4* for *h*. He searched the cryptogram for other words that contained these characters and found *;48;(88*, which he translated as follows:

t h e t (e e

But what did the symbol (stand for? To learn this he had to find the letter that completed the word, and only one fit. The symbol (stood for the letter *r*. The word was *tree*.

Now he knew the meaning of four characters. Adding to his store of letters in this way, he decoded the message the cryptogram concealed. But the message turned out to be a puzzle in its own right:

A good glass in the bishop's hostel in the devil's seat forty-one degrees and thirteen minutes northeast and by north main branch seventh limb east side shoot from the left eye of the death's-head a bee-line from the tree through the shot fifty feet out.

You will learn just how this message and the rare beetle were used to find a treasure if you read Edgar Allan Poe's wonderful story "The Gold-Bug."

In a village in England, a boy and his mother found a treasure map in an old sea chest. In the lower-left-hand corner of the map, an *X* appeared in red ink. Written next to it were the words "Bulk of treasure here." In the upper left were two more red *X*'s. On the back of the map were these notes:

Tall tree, spy-glass boulder bearing a point to N. of N.E. Skeleton Island E.S.E. by E.

Ten feet.

The bar silver is in the north cache; you can find it by the trend of the east hummock, ten fathoms south of the black crag with the face on it,

The arms are easy found, N. point of north inlet, bearing E. and a quarter N.

J.F.

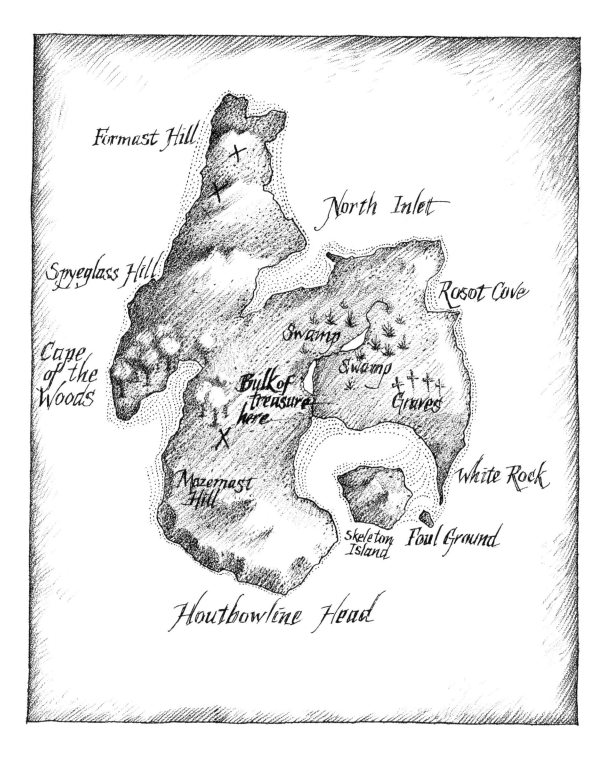

The notes were signed "J.F."

The boy took the map to the most important men in his village. From the initials "J.F." they knew it had belonged to a pirate captain, and they decided to search for the treasure.

Many treasure maps lead nowhere. Others lead not only to treasure but to adventures a treasure hunter never dreamed of. To learn what the men and the boy found when they followed this map, read Robert Louis Stevenson's book *Treasure Island*. To learn how this famous treasure map came to be, read pages 115–16 in the Notes in this book.

Treasure Island and "The Gold-Bug" are, of course, fiction. But often true stories are just as strange. In the real-life stories in this chapter, pinholes and shadow writing point the way to treasure, and so do a picture book for children and the Declaration of Independence.

Forty-five Pinholes

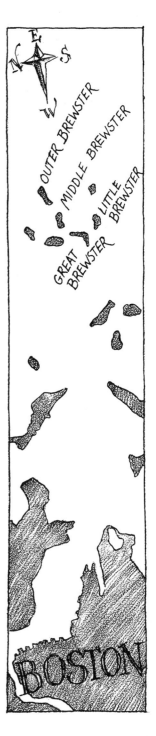

A TREASURE HUNTER NAMED EDWARD ROWE SNOW was on the trail of something hidden on an island in Boston Harbor. But he did not know exactly what he was looking for.

He had heard that in the late 1800s, a lighthouse keeper had hidden something, maybe a treasure, in an old house on one of the Brewster Islands.

This lighthouse keeper was a tall, fearsome-looking man named James Turner, with deep-set black eyes and a big black beard. Some people said that at one time Turner had been a pirate.

Snow went out to Great Brewster in his canoe to see what he could learn. There he met an old fisherman named John Nuskey, who remembered that years before, a man from Canada had spent two weeks on Great Brewster, looking for something he did not find.

When he left, the man wrote down what he was after and asked Nuskey to let him know if he came across it. The trouble was that Nuskey could not remember what he had done with the paper.

Six years later, he finally found it and showed it to Snow. It said:

> Write Thomas Redwick, General Delivery, Kingston,
> Ontario, if you find old book, cover of skin, message inside.
> In old sail in foundation of fisherman's house.

At last Snow knew what he was looking for. But there are *four* Brewster Islands. Besides Great Brewster, there are Little Brewster and Middle Brewster, which are connected to Great Brewster by sandbars. And there is Outer Brewster, which stands alone.

Since Redwick had not found anything on Great Brewster, Middle Brewster seemed like the best bet. On it, there was an old house near the verge of ruin, old enough for James Turner to have used. Nuskey told Snow he would go over and take a look, then let him know what he found.

But Snow never heard from him. A few days later, Nuskey's empty skiff floated ashore at Middle Brewster. A week after that, his body washed up on Nantasket Beach, to the south. Whether he died in an accident or in some other way was never decided.

Soon World War II came, and Snow went to fight overseas. When he returned several years later, he made plans to go out to Middle Brewster and continue his search. He had learned that a fisherman once lived in that old house on the island. It sounded more and more like the place Thomas Redwick had been after, and Snow got permission from the owner to look around.

After forcing open a trapdoor in the kitchen floor, he went down into the darkness of the cellar. In the corner he saw what looked like a pile of rags but was actually a piece of rotting canvas. He kicked at it, and the canvas fell apart. There was an old book underneath, just as Redwick had said. It had been printed in Italy in the year 1690.

Snow went through the book page by page, but found nothing that looked like the message Redwick had mentioned. He had the book translated from Italian, thinking that might help. But it turned out to be about the Catholic Church, not treasure.

Snow had a friend who was a librarian in the Rare Books Department at the Boston Public Library. He asked her to look at the book. Maybe she would see what he had missed. A week later, she telephoned. "Come in as soon as you can," she said. "I have something to show you."

A series of pinholes had been made over forty-five of the

letters on page 101. This clearly was what Redwick had been looking for. But what did it say?

Snow arranged the letters from each line side by side:

RABR

ETUOMAHT

AHCDN

ALSI

GNORT

SSEER

TTSA

EEUD

SIDLOG

But he saw no meaning in the list. He then tried working with the first letter in each line and got nowhere. Then he ran the nine lines of letters into one line in this way:

RABRETUOMAHTAHCDNALSIGNORTSSEERTTSAEEUDSIDLOG

It also meant nothing to him. He tried working with every second letter, then every third, but that did not achieve anything. He even tried the old trick of arranging the letters backward, like this:

GOLDISDUEEASTTREESSTRONGISLANDCHATHAMOUTERBAR

And he found what he was looking for!

GOLD IS DUE EAST TREES STRONG ISLAND
CHATHAM OUTER BAR

The following week, Snow went out to Strong Island, off Cape Cod. He lined up the trees with the outer sandbar, as the directions said. Then he started searching that section of the beach with a metal detector.

Months later, under five feet of sand, he uncovered a metal box with 316 gold coins in it—Spanish doubloons and pieces of eight, Portuguese moidores, and others.

Snow was elated, but puzzled. All treasures involve unanswered questions, but this one seemed to have more than its share. Why was it buried on Strong Island? If it was James Turner's treasure, where had he gotten it? Had he been a pirate, as people believed? Where did the old book come from? Who was Thomas Redwick? And what did John Nuskey's death have to do with it all? Snow never found the answers. Nor is it likely that anyone else will now.

Three Ciphers

ONE OF THE CIPHERS IN THIS STORY has already been solved. If you can solve one of the others, some say it will lead you to a $16 million treasure buried in Virginia.

The story of this treasure begins in 1817. A party of thirty men, led by Thomas Jefferson Beale, went out West to hunt. In Colorado, they discovered gold and silver and gave up hunting for mining.

After a year and a half, some of them took what they had found thus far back East. While the mining continued, Beale and ten men moved a half ton of gold and two tons of silver in horse-drawn wagons to Bufords, Virginia—now called Montvale—and buried it nearby. Then they went back to Colorado. Two years later, they returned to Bufords with another load. They buried it in the same place, along with a container of jewels.

On his two trips back to Virginia, Beale became friends with the owner of the hotel where he stayed, a man named Robert Morriss. Before he returned to Colorado a third time, he gave Morriss an iron box to keep for him. Later, he wrote to Morriss and told him to open the box if he did not come back within ten years.

Beale and his men were never heard from again. When Morriss finally opened the box, he found two letters from Beale and three ciphers, each made up of hundreds of numbers. In his letters, Beale told Morriss that the ciphers would lead him to a treasure.

When Morriss found the treasure, he was to divide it into thirty-one equal shares. He was to keep one share for himself and give the others to the families of the men who had gone West with Beale. Beale said that he would send the key to the ciphers by mail. But it had never arrived.

It is said that Morriss spent several years trying to solve the ciphers on his own, but could not break the code. Just before he died, in 1863, he gave them to his friend James Ward. Ward spent the next twenty years working on them. He became so obsessed with solving the ciphers that he neglected his business and almost went broke.

He finally succeeded in solving cipher number 2, which describes the treasure. This was the message it contained:

> I have deposited in the county of Bedford about four miles from Bufords in an excavation or vault six feet below the surface of the ground the following articles belonging jointly to the parties whose names are given in [Cipher] Number Three. . . .
>
> The first deposit consisted of ten hundred and fourteen pounds of gold and thirty-eight hundred and twelve pounds of silver deposited Nov eighteen hundred and nineteen. The second deposit was made Dec eighteen twenty-one and consisted of nineteen hundred and seven pounds of gold and twelve hundred and eighty-eight of silver. Also, jewels obtained in St. Louis in exchange for gold . . . and valued at thirteen thousand dollars.
>
> The above is securely packed in iron pots with iron

covers. The vault is roughly lined with stone, and the vessels rest on solid stone and are covered with others.

[Cipher] Number One describes the exact locality of the vault . . .

Ward is said to have solved this cipher when he discovered that it was based on the 1,322 words in the Declaration of Independence. Whoever created the cipher numbered the words in the Declaration in the order of their appearance, then gave the number of each word to the first letter in that word.

Since "events" is the seventh word in the Declaration, its first letter, *e*, was given the number 7. When *e* was the first letter of another word, that letter *e* was given the number of its word. So *e* appears in the cipher as several numbers— *7, 37, 49,* and others.

Here is how the first words in cipher number 2 were decoded:

115	73	24	818	37	52	49	17	31	62	657	22	7	15
I	h	a	v	e	d	e	p	o	s	i	t	e	d

Ward spent the next two years trying to solve cipher number 1, which is supposed to give the location of the treasure, and cipher number 3, a list of those who were to get the treasure. Cipher number 1 is, of course, the one to concentrate on. It is on page 64. Ciphers number 2 and number 3 are on pages 118 and 119 in the Notes.

Over the years, there have been hundreds of solutions to ciphers number 1 and number 3. None has been correct, but treasure hunters keep trying. These days, most use computers, but they also search old records, newspaper files, and histories for leads.

Some say the whole thing is a hoax. But computer experts say that the ciphers, at least, are real and do have solutions.

There is even a Beale Cypher Association, which has been

Cipher number 1: The location of the treasure

71	194	38	1701	89	76	11	83	1629	48
94	63	132	16	111	95	84	341	975	14
40	64	27	81	139	213	63	90	1120	8
15	3	126	2018	40	74	758	485	604	230
436	664	582	150	251	284	308	231	124	211
486	225	401	370	11	101	305	139	189	17
33	88	208	193	145	1	94	73	416	918
263	28	500	538	356	117	136	219	27	176
130	10	460	25	485	18	436	65	84	200
283	118	320	138	36	416	280	15	71	224
961	44	16	401	39	88	61	304	12	21
24	283	134	92	63	246	486	682	7	219
184	360	780	18	64	463	474	131	160	79
73	440	95	18	64	581	34	69	128	367
460	17	81	12	103	820	62	116	97	103
862	70	60	1317	471	540	208	121	890	346
36	150	59	568	614	13	120	63	219	812
2160	1780	99	35	18	21	136	872	15	28
170	88	4	30	44	112	18	147	436	195
320	37	122	113	6	140	8	120	305	42
58	461	44	106	301	13	408	680	93	86
116	530	82	568	9	102	38	416	89	71
216	728	965	818	2	38	121	195	14	326
148	234	18	55	131	234	361	824	5	81
623	48	961	19	26	33	10	1101	365	92
88	181	275	346	201	206	86	36	219	320
829	840	68	326	19	48	122	85	216	284
919	861	326	985	233	64	68	232	431	960
50	29	81	216	321	603	14	612	81	360
36	51	62	194	78	60	200	314	676	112
4	28	18	61	136	247	819	921	1060	464
895	10	6	66	119	38	41	49	602	423
962	302	294	875	78	14	23	111	109	62
31	501	823	216	280	34	24	150	1000	162
286	19	21	17	340	19	242	31	86	234
140	607	115	33	191	67	104	86	52	88
16	80	121	67	95	122	216	548	96	11
201	77	364	218	65	667	890	236	154	211
10	98	34	119	56	216	119	71	218	1164
1496	1817	51	39	210	36	3	19	540	232
22	141	617	84	290	80	46	207	411	150
29	38	46	172	85	194	36	261	543	897
624	18	212	416	127	931	19	4	63	96
12	101	418	16	140	230	460	538	19	27
88	612	1431	90	716	275	74	83	11	426
89	72	84	1300	1706	814	221	132	40	102
34	858	975	1101	84	16	79	23	16	81
122	324	403	912	227	936	447	55	86	34
43	212	107	96	314	264	1065	323	428	601
203	124	95	216	814	2906	654	820	2	301
112	176	213	71	87	96	202	35	10	2
41	17	84	221	736	820	214	11	60	760

organized to solve the ciphers and recover the treasure, if there is one. If you would like more information on the ciphers, see the association's address on page 116 in the Notes.

The Arrows and the Ring

A BOY WALKING NEAR THE RIO GRANDE IN TEXAS late one summer afternoon saw a giant arrow on the ridge of a hill. The arrow pointed south. Soon he saw another, like the first, pointing down the hill. Then he came upon a large ring of rocks in a hollow.

When he told his father what he had seen, his father got excited. He said they were treasure signs. The arrows pointed to the ring of rocks, and the ring was where you were supposed to dig.

But when they went back the next morning with shovels, they could not find the arrows. They looked all over, but the arrows had disappeared, and without them they could not find the ring. They searched again and again but found nothing.

What they did not know was that the pieces of wood or rock that had been arranged as arrows could be seen *only* when they cast shadows. And that depended on the position of the sun. And that depended not only on the time of day but on the season of the year. Only those who had been told beforehand knew just when and where to look for the arrows.

When the boy became a man, he learned that years before, Spanish explorers had used this method to give secret directions to treasure they had hidden. He went back and searched for the arrows again, but the season and the time were not right.

Many such signs were used to point the way to hidden

treasures. They were marked or carved on stones, rocks, cliffs, trees, and cactus plants. Or they were formed from stones or pieces of wood. Of course, you had to know what they were, or you ignored them. Here are some that you might see—or put to use one day.

The treasure is this way. An arrow, a snake, or a turtle points in the right direction.

The treasure has been buried in two places.

You are on the right trail. A large eye was sometimes used as a trail marker. So were an X or the figures *3* or *7*.

The treasure is inside a cave.

The treasure is inside a triangle formed by rocks or trees.

The treasure is in a box or chest.

A gold or silver mine is nearby. The sun shining is the sign for this.

Dig on the other side of this tree. A snake crawling up a tree is the sign.

Dig below. A coiled snake drawn on a rock was used. So was a drawing of a mule's shoe, with the closed end down or a semicircle with a dot in the center.

A Golden Rabbit

THE MOON HAD FALLEN IN LOVE WITH THE SUN. As a token of its love, it sent the sun a piece of jewelry, a golden rabbit. A real rabbit carried the gift. But on its way to the sun, the rabbit lost it. Where had the golden rabbit gone?

This was the story and the puzzle of an English picture book called *Masquerade*. The author was an artist named Kit Williams, a smallish man with a big red beard.

The book involved a real treasure hunt. If you were the first to solve the puzzle, you would find a golden rabbit. Williams had made one and decorated it with rubies, moonstones, and other gems. By the time he finished, it was worth over ten thousand dollars.

Then he hid it. He placed it in a ceramic box, covered the box with wax to protect it, and put it in an earthenware jar. On an August night when the moon was full, he buried the jar fourteen inches underground somewhere in the British Isles.

All the clues needed to find the rabbit were in his book. Some were in the story. Others were shown in the pictures. In fact, a person could win the rabbit by staying home and studying the book. If someone found the answer, Williams would take him or her to the treasure and help to dig it up.

But thousands went out and hunted the golden rabbit themselves. They spent their nights searching the book for clues and plotting their strategy with maps and diagrams. On weekends, they dug holes all over the British Isles. They used picks, shovels, metal detectors, climbing ropes, even rubber dinghies. One person came within seventy feet of the treasure—then went off in the wrong direction.

Although *Masquerade* was intended for children, a great many of the searchers were adults. The book became so

popular, it sold over a million copies. One man said he would bury the treasure again if he found it. He just liked the idea of the hunt going on and on.

A forty-eight-year-old engineer finally found the rabbit, eighteen months after he began looking for it. He dug it up on a wintry February night in a small park in the village of Ampthill, thirty-five miles from London.

A clue under the first picture in the book started him toward the treasure. It consisted of five words: "one of six to eight." It stood for Queen Katharine of Aragon, the first of six wives to King Henry VIII. The engineer figured that out soon after he read the book.

Then, he wasted a whole year hunting for the rabbit near the castle where Katharine had died, following what he thought were clues in the book. He twice became so discouraged that he gave away his copy. Each time, he bought a new one and searched it again for clues.

Then he found a shortcut. He read elsewhere that the author of the book had lived in Ampthill as a child. When he found that Katharine also had lived there, he decided *that* was where the golden rabbit was buried.

He went to Ampthill with a friend to search, but they could not find a sign of the treasure. Fortunately, he had his dog with him. Before leaving, he took it to a park, and the dog ran off to find a tree. While waiting, the man noticed a small stone cross honoring Queen Katharine.

Cut in the stone were these words from the 104th Psalm: ". . . the earth is full of Thy riches." He turned to his friend and cried, "The rabbit could be here!"

But just where was "here"? He went back to the book and found the answer in the second picture. It showed a man and a woman, who stood for the sun and the moon, dancing together. Their hands were clasped so that they pointed to a date on a calendar.

It was March 21, the date of the spring equinox, when day and night are of equal length. At some time on that day, the engineer decided, the shadow cast by the stone cross would point to where the golden rabbit was buried.

But he could not wait until March 21. That was a month away, and he feared that someone might beat him to the treasure. He began visiting the park at night, to avoid the prying eyes of other treasure hunters. Using his flashlight as the sun, he dug holes wherever it seemed that the shadow of the cross might fall on the day of the equinox. On the night of February 24, he found the right spot.

7

THE NEEDLE IN A HAYSTACK

When you know for certain that a treasure ship sank somewhere off the Marquesas Atolls or that a lost mine is not far from a big rock shaped like a sombrero, you have found the haystack. The problem then is finding the needle.

To do that, you need not only facts but good luck. You could search to the left instead of the right or dig down three feet instead of four feet and miss the treasure completely.

Finally, there is the problem of removing the treasure from the swamp or pit or ocean bottom where it has been found, which often is not easy.

To find the needle and bring it back, treasure hunters have depended on all sorts of things over the years—divining rods, rakes and tongs, diving bells, derricks, baby submarines, sonar, metal detectors, and, of course, good luck.

Doctor Knipperhausen
and His Divining Rod

WOLFERT WEBBER HELD THE LANTERN. Dressed in a cloak and a black velvet cap, Doctor Knipperhausen held the divining rod. It was a small forked branch he had cut from a tree. A fisherman named Sam stood nearby with a shovel, ready to dig.

The doctor grasped the forked ends of the branch firmly, with the stem pointing up. He moved from place to place, holding the branch at about the height of his shoulders. From time to time, he closed his eyes in concentration.

Soon the divining rod began to twist and turn, as if it had a mind of its own. When the stem pointed toward the ground, it stopped moving.

"This is the spot," the doctor said, in a voice that could scarcely be heard. He made a small fire and cast dried herbs into it, muttering conjuring rituals in German. Buried treasure was thought to be controlled by the devil, and these rituals were to keep him at bay. Then Doctor Knipperhausen told Sam to start digging.

If you read Washington Irving's story "Wolfert Webber, or Golden Dreams," you will learn how Wolfert, Doctor Knipperhausen, and Sam found treasure with a divining rod, then lost it in a mysterious and startling way.

Doctor Knipperhausen's divining rod was not his invention, of course. For hundreds of years it was the only equipment treasure hunters had to find buried treasure.

The branch of a divining rod was always cut from a special

tree, usually a hazel, a willow, or a holly. Even then, not everybody could make it work, only those who, it was said, had the "gift."

A few treasure hunters still use divining rods to hunt for gold. Others use them to search for sources of water underground. But researchers say that a divining rod does not work by itself. As it twists and turns, it may express a person's subconscious reactions to what he sees as he searches. When the stem of the branch points to the ground, the person may have seen enough to believe that this is where a treasure is buried. Either that, or the person is guessing.

Captain Phips and His Fantastic Good Luck

ALONG THE WATERFRONT IN BOSTON, Captain William Phips had often heard of the fleet of treasure ships that had gone down in the West Indies. They had sunk somewhere north of the island of Hispaniola, which today we call Santo Domingo.

When Phips sailed to Hispaniola to see for himself, in 1683, an old Portuguese sailor he had met in Porto de Plata told him that the story was true. Forty years earlier, Spanish galleons had crashed into a reef and sunk. The man had seen the survivors from one ship come ashore on a raft, and nobody had touched the wreck since.

Why had he not gone after it himself, Phips asked the sailor. How could he, with no ship and no money, he replied. And others, why did they not search? They were fools, the sailor said.

If Phips was interested, the wreck was just a few leagues to the north, near Turks Island and the Handkerchief Shoals.

Phips searched the reefs and shoals to the north and found nothing. Without the exact latitude, finding the wreck seemed hopeless.

Four years later, he came back to search again, this time in an area of reefs and shoals to the southeast. Working from canoes, Indian skin divers he had hired and his own crew searched one reef after another. When evening fell, they would go back to the ship they used as a base, then they would return in the morning to try again. After weeks of searching, they gave up.

As the divers moved away from the last reef, they saw below, in the clear blue-green water, a beautiful pale-red plant called a sea feather. Phips, who had stayed behind in Porto de Plata, would be disappointed that they had found nothing, and they thought the plant might cheer him up.

One of the men dived into the water for it and saw, on the bottom, a bronze cannon! He had found a treasure ship! The ship was wedged between two rocks, and after forty years it was almost completely covered with coral.

Over the next three days, divers brought up three thousand pieces of eight and dozens of ingots of silver, some weighing over two hundred pounds.

The crew decided it would be fun to surprise Phips. When they got back to Porto de Plata, they gave him the sea feather and told him they had found nothing else. He was so discouraged, he said finding the treasure was impossible. As they talked, someone slipped an ingot of silver under Phips' table. Suddenly he saw it.

"Why, what is this?" he asked. "Whence comes this?" When they told him, he said, "Then thanks be to God! We are made!" The treasure was not just a "few leagues" from Porto de Plata, as he had been told, but twenty-eight leagues, or eighty-four miles.

Phips anchored his two ships, the *Henry* and the *James and Mary*, as close as he could to the reef where the wreck had

been found. He then sent out a fleet of canoes and other boats, from which the skin divers explored the remains of the galleon.

Using a rope attached to a boat as a guide, and a rock as a weight, they dropped to the bottom of the sea. Holding their breath as long as possible, they sent up baskets and nets of coins and other treasure. It was a technique pearl divers and sponge divers used all over the world. Some also took down diving buckets they held upside down. This trapped air they could gulp, which helped them to stay under a little longer.

Meanwhile, sailors in the boats reached into the water with long-handled rakes to comb the sea bottom and with tongs to pick up whatever they found.

"Fishing the wreck," the crew called it. In the six weeks they fished the wreck, they brought up over thirty-two tons of gold and silver.

Doctor Halley and His Diving Bell

A FEW YEARS AFTER WILLIAM PHIPS FOUND HIS TREASURE, the scientist Edmund Halley invented the diving bell and diving suit shown in the drawing. He was the man who earlier had discovered Halley's Comet. His diving bell and diving suit made it possible for a diver to spend a whole hour under water instead of just a few minutes.

The bell enabled the diver to rest while breathing fresh air. The air was in a lead barrel that had been lowered to the ocean floor. It then flowed through an oiled leather pipe to the bell. The bell was open at the bottom to allow a diver to enter and leave, but the air inside kept the water out.

The diving suit consisted of a lead helmet with a glass

window and a leather coverall something like a jumpsuit. A second leather pipe brought fresh air from the diving bell to the helmet. A third pipe allowed used air to escape through the diving suit.

Next, Halley invented a device that blew up the decks of sunken ships, making it easier to get at treasure inside. He formed a business that used all this equipment to hunt sunken treasure around the British Isles.

Captain Dickinson and His Giant Derrick

SOUTHEAST OF RIO DE JANEIRO, the rugged cliffs of Cape Frio rise one hundred and fifty feet straight up out of the ocean. There are no beaches and harbors, only strong winds and turbulent waters. At the base of these stern headlands, the ocean is thirty to seventy feet deep.

On the night of December 4, 1830, in a blinding rainstorm, the British frigate *Thetis* was moving east under full sail, with 800,000 dollars in gold and silver coins.* It lost its way and crashed at high speed into this wall of stone.

Most of the crew of three hundred were killed. By some miracle, a few escaped to a narrow ledge in the rock and rescued others trapped on board. Mountainous waves hurled the wreck of the *Thetis* against the cliffs again and again, then drove it into a tiny cove a third of a mile away, where it sank with the treasure.

When news of the wreck reached Rio, the British warship *Lightning* and four other vessels went to help. They removed the survivors, but recovering the treasure seemed impossible.

* The English called various South American coins dollars.

However, Captain Thomas Dickinson of the *Lightning* insisted he could do it and was given permission to try.

Dickinson planned to use a diving bell to find the treasure and bring it to the surface. Under normal conditions, the bell would be lowered with a block and tackle from a ship. But in the angry winds and waters of Cape Frio, there was a great risk that anchors would not hold, and the ship would be driven into the cliffs.

Instead, Dickinson decided to install a derrick in the cove where the *Thetis* sank. The diving bell would hang from the end of it like a weight on the end of a fishing pole. They would use chains and cables to lower and raise the derrick and move it from side to side. In this way they could place the bell where they wanted it, then lift it out.

But there wasn't a diving bell or a derrick in the area. Dickinson's crew would have to build them from what they could find. After the *Lightning* returned to Rio, they cut and shaped a diving bell from two iron tanks, then from odds and ends built an air pump to operate it.

The makeshift bell was similar to the one Edmund Halley had invented. (There is a drawing of Halley's bell on page 78.) It did not have a glass top, but it was open at the bottom. This enabled the crew to look through the opening for treasure and reach out to recover what they saw. A stream of air pumped from above would provide the oxygen they needed and also keep water from coming in.

Dickinson went back to Cape Frio with the diving bell and the air pump. His crew set up camp about a mile from the headlands and began to assemble the huge arm of the derrick. Since there was no timber, they used the masts and spars that had floated ashore from the wreck of the *Thetis*.

Other crew members leveled a platform for the derrick and its operating gear on a piece of rock about forty feet above the cove. To lower and raise the derrick, they would use chains and cables, with windlasses to wind them up and release them. To support the windlasses, they built platforms on the cliffs above. But before the equipment could be installed, roads and footpaths to each of the platforms had to be cut in the stone.

While all this was going on, storms scattered the wreckage of the *Thetis*. Dickinson was no longer sure just where in the cove the treasure lay. To install the derrick in the right position, it was something he needed to know.

Despite the risk from rough seas, he decided to launch a second, smaller diving bell to search for the wreckage. His crew made the bell from an old water tank. It was just a little black pot, barely big enough for two men. A boat would drop it over the side, then haul it up when the divers were ready to move on.

The first time they launched the bell, ten-foot waves turned it over and filled it with water. The divers escaped, and the search went on. After they had explored the bottom of the cove for several days, up bobbed a piece of wood. On it was written: ". . . we are now over some dollars." When the bell was hauled up, the divers crawled out holding their caps, which were overflowing with gold and silver coins.

When the crew had finished the arm of the derrick, it was one hundred and fifty-eight feet long, over half the length of a football field. It consisted of twenty-two pieces of wood held together with dowels, iron bolts, hoops, and wrappings of four-inch rope. With its operating gear, it would weigh almost forty tons.

They placed the arm in the ocean and towed it to the cove. Three days later, the derrick was in position on top of the cliff. They attached the big diving bell and were ready to begin operations. In the weeks that followed, divers recovered 130,000 dollars in treasure from the floor of the cove. Then a terrific storm roared in. It tore the derrick apart and sent the bell and its air pump crashing into the ocean.

Captain Dickinson did not give up. When the storm ended, his men stretched a cable across the cove, built still another diving bell, and suspended it from the cable. By lowering and raising the cable, they could lower and raise the bell as they had done before. They found the air pump on the bottom of the cove and went back to work.

Over fourteen months, they brought up almost all of the treasure that went under on that terrible night when the *Thetis* lost its way.

Simon Lake's Baby Submarine

A HUNDRED YEARS AFTER THOMAS DICKINSON built his giant derrick, Simon Lake built a miniature submarine. In 1935, he used it for a treasure hunt on the bottom of the East River in New York.

The famous submarine inventor was searching for the

remains of the British warship *Hussar*. The ship had struck a rock and sunk in 1780, during the American Revolution, not far from what today is the south Bronx.

The *Hussar* was said to be carrying five million dollars' worth of gold coins to Newport, Rhode Island, to pay the British troops stationed there. Fifty American prisoners of war who were locked in the hold drowned. Lake was certain from his research that the *Hussar* was somewhere in the river between 130th and 136th Streets.

The submarine he used to explore the river bottom was only twenty-two feet long, just a little longer than a station wagon. It moved along the bottom on thirty-inch iron wheels and was equipped with two floodlights, and a crane to lift whatever it found. It also had an air lock, which allowed divers to leave and return to the sub underwater.

The baby sub worked perfectly, and Lake used it for over a year in his search. Yet he found no trace of the *Hussar*. Some thought that what remained of the ship was buried in a part of the river that had been filled in as a foundation for an apartment house. As you will see in the next section, they may have been wrong.

Echoes and Beeps

THREE INVENTIONS FROM WORLD WAR II that were designed to attack an enemy are now used to find treasure.

One is scuba, which stands for *s*elf-*c*ontained *u*nderwater *b*reathing *a*pparatus. Naval divers, or frogmen, used it to help blow up enemy ships and carry out espionage. Now skin divers use it to explore the ocean bottom for signs of treasure.

It consists of a tank of compressed air a diver wears on his back that feeds oxygen to a mouthpiece, through which he breathes. With this equipment and a wet suit and flippers, he can swim as deep as a hundred feet for as long as an hour.

Sonar is another of these wartime inventions. It was designed to track enemy submarines. But treasure hunters use it to help find sunken ships. As they tow a sonar device behind a search boat, it fires electrical impulses into the water. These impulses bounce off whatever they hit and send back echoes. The echoes are picked up by a recorder, which uses them to outline what the object looks like.

In 1984, a band of treasure hunters from Nevada used sonar to find the remains of the British sloop of war *De Braek*. Loaded with booty from Spanish ships, it had sunk two hundred years before, two miles off the coast of Delaware.

Sonar was used in 1985 to find what appeared to be the British warship *Hussar*, for which Simon Lake had searched in vain fifty years before in his baby submarine. The vessel lay in eighty feet of water in New York Harbor, off a treacherous passage called Hell Gate.

It was located by the treasure hunter Barry Clifford, who earlier had found the pirate ship *Whydah*, a story told in Chapter 3. Clifford spent two years searching for the *Hussar*. "Just as I said, 'This is where it is,' the ship popped up on the screen," he told reporters.

The mine detector was the third of these inventions. It looked like a floor polisher, but it dealt with life and death. Its purpose was to locate buried land mines before soldiers advancing into battle set them off. Often a party of soldiers called mine sweepers went first on foot, moving mine detectors back and forth across the ground. Whenever a detector passed over a mine, it buzzed or sounded some other warning.

Treasure hunters now use similar equipment to find metal objects as deep as twenty feet underground. Today the equipment is called a metal detector or magnetometer—mag, for short. Except for an accurate treasure map, a mag is the most useful tool treasure hunters have ever had.

When Edward Rowe Snow used a metal detector in 1945 to help find a buried treasure, he probably was the first to do so. (That story is told in "Forty-five Pinholes," in Chapter 6.) Hundreds of thousands of treasure hunters now use metal detectors to scour fields, beaches, and deserts for old coins and other riches.

Those who are after sunken treasure tow a detector behind their search craft, as they might tow a sonar device. Often the two are used together. The sonar locates what is on the ocean floor, and the metal detector points to what is buried below.

The first underwater detectors could only find objects made from iron, like cannonballs, tools, and bolts. They helped to locate the remains of treasure ships, but not their gold or silver that had been scattered.

You may recall from the story in Chapter 3 that Mel Fisher used such equipment in his search for the *Atocha* and the *Santa Margarita*. Each time a strong "hit" was registered, a skin diver went down to see what had caused it. It was a painstaking process, and it took years. But without a metal detector, Fisher never would have found the two galleons.

Toward the end of Fisher's search, a detector was invented that found gold, silver, and bronze, as well as iron. It was small enough so that a diver could hold it in his hand. Using it as he swam above the ocean floor, one of Fisher's divers found what he thought was an old can under four feet of sand. It turned out to be a jewel box. Inside were two million dollars' worth of jewels.

8

THE CURIOUS TREASURE
OF CAPTAIN KIDD

My name is Captain Kidd.
What the law did forbid
Unluckily I did
*   when I sailed.*

Upon the ocean wide
I robbed on every side
With the most ambitious pride
*   when I sailed . . .*

Captain Kidd was said to be the most famous pirate in the Western world. Ballads were written about him, like the one above. People still believe that he brought home a fabulous treasure from his plunderings and buried it somewhere on the east coast of North America.

Over the years, treasure hunters have dug for it on Oak Island in Nova Scotia; on Jesse Hadley's farm in Weare, New Hampshire; along the Hudson River in New York; on Clarke's Island near Northfield, Massachusetts; on Block Island, off Rhode Island; in Shark

River, New Jersey; in Lewes, Delaware; and in hundreds of other places. But no one has found it.

Much of what we know of Captain Kidd has come down to us through song and story. But was he really a pirate? And did he really bury a treasure, or have tens of thousands of people searched in vain? It is a tangled tale of mutiny, piracy, murder, treachery—and gold and silver.

CAPTAIN WILLIAM KIDD WAS A SHIPMASTER in New York City in the 1690s, when New York was an English colony. He lived with his wife and children in a big house on Liberty Street.

If anyone had accused Kidd of piracy, those who knew him would have laughed. He was widely thought of as a decent, trustworthy man. In fact, he once had worked for the colonial government tracking down pirates in the waters around New York.

In those days, pirates plundered British ships wherever they found them. It was such a problem that the King of England decided to crush them once and for all, and he ordered the Royal Governor of New York, the Earl of Bellomont, to do so.

Governor Bellomont asked Kidd to take on the job. His orders were to capture as many pirates and pirate ships as he could in two years. He also was to capture any French ships he saw, because England was at war with France.

Bellomont bought Kidd a ship, the *Adventure Galley*, and armed it with thirty-four cannons. Kidd was to hire a crew. But there would be no money to pay them. Instead, they would get one-fourth of any booty they took from the pirates or the French. If they took no booty, they would get no pay. Since few seamen would work under such conditions, Kidd could hire only wastrels and drifters, some of whom were former pirates.

He left New York in September 1696 with one hundred

and fifty-five men and sailed to the Madeira Islands off Africa. He continued south around the tip of Africa, into the Indian Ocean. Then he headed north toward the island of Madagascar, where many pirates made their headquarters. But Kidd did not find any.

In the five months since he'd left New York, he had not taken any booty, and his crew had not been paid. Frustrated and angry, they threatened to mutiny. But Kidd quieted them with talk of the dazzling riches that lay ahead. They set sail for the coast of India, where he hoped to find pirates.

Soon they came upon a merchant ship, the *Loyal Captain*. When she turned out to be a Dutch vessel, Kidd decided to send her on her way. But his crew had other ideas. They grabbed the guns on board and got ready to steal whatever she had.

"Let's take her!" they yelled.

"No!" Kidd cried. "She is not our enemy."

"We'll take her anyway!"

"Desert my ship," he warned, "and I'll turn my cannons on you."

The mutiny died. But in a week or two, Kidd clashed with one of its leaders, a gunner named William Moore. Moore blamed him for not taking any ships. "You have brought us ruin," he snarled. Kidd struck him on the head with a bucket and killed him. The crew muttered and rumbled like distant thunder, but did nothing. Later, the ballad writer wrote:

> *Many long leagues from shore*
> *I murdered William Moore*
> *And laid him in his gore*
> *   when I sailed.*

The *Adventure Galley* and its crew sailed on. They came to a French ship that had been wrecked. Since France and England were at war, Kidd took what gold there was and shared it with his men. But this did not satisfy them. They continued to threaten him. They wanted him to attack every ship they saw, not just French or pirate ships.

Fearing for his life, Kidd finally gave in. He and his crew plundered several small vessels. Then they took a large merchant ship, the *November*, which was loaded with cotton and sugar. Two months later, they captured the *Quedah Merchant*, with a cargo of gold, silver, jewels, silk, and other goods.

Both were owned by the Great Mogul, the Emperor of India. The Mogul traded with England, but he also traded with her enemy, France. When Kidd checked the papers of the two ships, he breathed a sigh of relief. He found that France had agreed to protect them as if they were French ships. Under his orders, it seemed that he could take them as prizes of war. Kidd kept their "French papers" as proof that he had done the right thing, even if he had done so by accident.

When the *Adventure Galley* sprung a leak, he set sail for the port of St. Marie in Madagascar and took the Mogul's ships with him. What happened to their crews is not known. But on the way, some of Kidd's crew mutinied again. They stole what they could from the *November*, then sank it.

When Kidd and his men arrived at St. Marie, the *Adventure Galley* was leaking badly. To add to his troubles, Kidd found a pirate ship, the *Mocha Frigate*, tied up there. Kidd ordered the pirates to surrender, but they fled into the woods.

He told his crew to go after them, but most decided to join the pirates. They brought the pirates back from where they were hiding, then gave Kidd his choice of also turning pirate or losing his life.

He locked himself in his cabin on the *Adventure Galley*, loaded forty pistols, and waited for them to attack. Instead, they boarded Kidd's other ship, the *Quedah Merchant*, moved part of her cargo to the *Mocha Frigate*, and sailed away. But in their haste they left behind a treasure trove of gold, silver, and jewels.

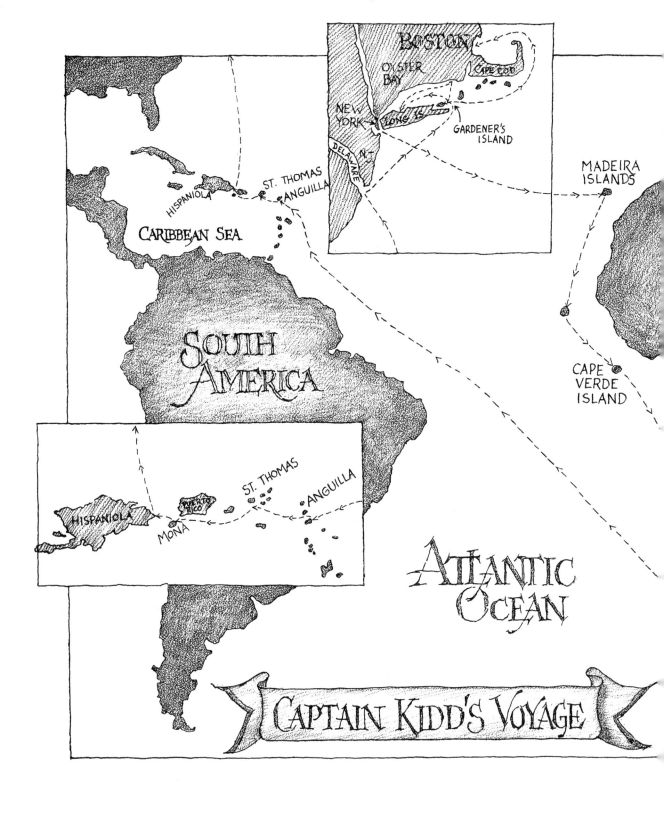

BOSTON

OYSTER
BAY

CAPE COD

NEW
YORK

LONG IS.

GARDENER'S
ISLAND

N.J.

DELAWARE

MADEIRA
ISLANDS

ST. THOMAS

ANGUILLA

HISPANIOLA

CARIBBEAN SEA

CAPE
VERDE
ISLAND

SOUTH
AMERICA

ST. THOMAS

ANGUILLA

HISPANIOLA

PUERTO
RICO

MONA

ATLANTIC
OCEAN

CAPTAIN KIDD'S VOYAGE

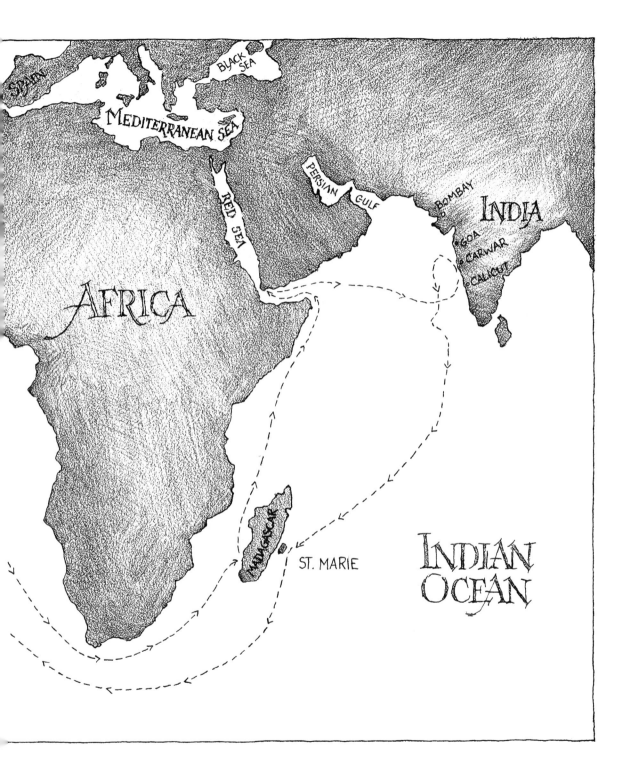

When the *Adventure Galley* began to sink where it was anchored, Kidd burned it. He then set sail for home in the *Quedah Merchant* with the seamen who had remained loyal. It was two and a half years since he had left New York.

Meanwhile, the Great Mogul had complained to England that Kidd had stolen his ships. The English quickly charged Kidd with piracy. It was a crime that carried the penalty of death, and they began to hunt him down. Only when he stopped for supplies in the West Indies did he learn that he was a hunted man.

Kidd was not sure that he could count on Governor Bellomont to help clear him. As insurance, he bought a sloop called the *San Antonio*, and with this new ship and the *Quedah Merchant*, he sailed to Hispaniola. There he moved the treasure from the *Quedah Merchant* to the *San Antonio*. He hid the *Quedah Merchant* and the rest of its cargo in a small cove and left part of his crew to guard it. If he needed to, he would try to trade the ship for a pardon from the charge of piracy.

Kidd sailed north on the *San Antonio* to Delaware Bay, where he stopped for supplies. Then he moved on toward New York City, anchoring nearby at Oyster Bay. He sent a note to his wife and a letter to a lawyer named James Emmot, who had defended other men charged with piracy. Would he see Governor Bellomont for him?

Emmot agreed to do so, and he and Kidd met on the *San Antonio*. Kidd told him that he was not a pirate, that he had taken the Mogul's ships as part of England's war with France. He gave him the French papers to show Bellomont as proof of this.

Since Bellomont was in Boston, Kidd sailed with Emmot to Rhode Island. There he put him ashore, and the lawyer made his way by land to see the governor. Kidd waited on the *San Antonio*.

Emmot returned in a few days. He had left the French papers with Bellomont as evidence of Kidd's innocence. And he had brought back a letter. Bellomont had written to Kidd: "If you are telling the truth, you will be safe from arrest. Come ashore and meet with me in Boston."

Kidd decided to see Bellomont, but he still did not completely trust him. He decided to leave the treasure aboard the *San Antonio* in a safe place. He sailed to Gardiner's Island, in Long Island Sound, a hundred miles from New York City. There he left Emmot to make his way home, then he talked the owner of the island, a man named John Gardiner, into keeping part of the treasure for him. Gardiner buried it on the island. Some of Kidd's friends came aboard the *San Antonio* and took away the rest. Only then did Kidd set sail for Boston to see Bellomont.

But Bellomont had lied to him. When Kidd went ashore, he was arrested and sent to England in chains, to be tried for piracy. Bellomont told Kidd he had to arrest him. But he said he would send the French papers to England so that Kidd could use them at his trial. Whether he would keep his word this time remained to be seen.

Bellomont quickly seized the buried treasure on Gardiner's Island, as well as the treasure Kidd had given his friends to keep for him. It came to sixty-eight pounds of gold, one hundred and forty-three pounds of silver, and a pound of rubies, diamonds, and other jewels. Today the gold and silver alone would be worth half a million dollars. The governor also sent a crew to find the *Quedah Merchant* and its cargo.

At his trial in London, Kidd demanded the French papers Bellomont had promised to send. They were the only chance he had to save his life. But the government said there were no such papers, and Kidd was sentenced to hang for piracy.

It was the most famous trial of the day. As most people saw it, Kidd was a good man who had gone bad. The wildest tales were told of how wicked he had become and how much wealth he had. The ballad writer wrote of him:

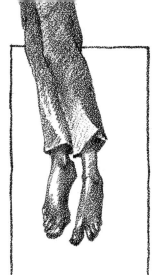

I steered from sound to sound
And many ships I found
And most of them I burned
*   as I sailed . . .*

I had ninety bars of gold
And dollars manifold
With riches uncontrolled
*   as I sailed.*

Captain Kidd rode to his execution, standing backward in a cart, a noose around his neck. Huge crowds jeered and pelted him with rubbish and rocks as he passed.

He was hanged three times. The first time the rope broke. So he was hanged a second time. Then his body was covered with tar and taken to the waterfront, where it was hung from another gallows—a warning to seamen on passing ships not to become pirates.

There the story ends, and we return to the questions at the beginning of this chapter. Was Kidd really a pirate? And was there really a buried treasure?

There was a treasure, as we have seen, but it was buried for only a few weeks. Yet few knew it had been found, and people searched for it for more than two hundred years.

Whether Kidd was really a pirate is something that you must decide for yourself. Did he take the ships he captured because his crew forced him to do so? Or did he take them out of greed? Or was it both? Through song and story, Kidd became the symbol of every pirate. And his treasure, for which people searched so long, became the symbol of every treasure.

9

NO GOOD CAME OF IT

There are times when it would have been far better if a treasure had never been found. For all the riches involved, no good came of it.

The Message

SANDY DUGUID WAS A FISHERMAN who lived on Norton's Point in Penobscot Bay, Maine, early in the nineteenth century. One day, he came upon three cairns of rock that together formed a triangle. "Pirate's treasure!" he thought.

As tradition had taught him to do, he located the center of the triangle, and there he dug. Under a flat rock he found a wooden chest filled with Spanish coins of gold and silver. There was also this message, written on a piece of parchment:

A curse on the man who removes this chest and upon the region. Let him beware.

Misfortune will follow him to the end of his days.

Duguid laughed. It was all nonsense, he told his friends. But from that day on, nothing seemed to go right for him. Storms washed away his fishing nets and lobster traps. Blight and frost ruined his vegetable garden and fruit trees. An illness no one understood crippled him. Then lightning hit his house and burned it to the ground.

Years later, Patrick Collins built a house where Sandy Duguid's house once stood. Storms, blight, and illness dogged him as they had Duguid. Then lightning hit *his* house and burned it to the ground.

Still later, a man searching where the two houses had stood found an old Spanish coin that Duguid probably had lost. On his way home, he passed a granite quarry just as dynamite was set off to free some rock. A piece of flying granite hit his leg and injured it so badly it had to be amputated.

Soon after, a friend who worked in that quarry borrowed the coin to study it. The next day, he was caught in a blast that blinded him for life. Later, another friend borrowed it to show to his wife, and he went mad.

Many years after these incidents, a college professor got hold of the coin for the museum at his school. He had been vacationing on an island in Penobscot Bay and had the coin with him when he returned to the mainland. The ship he was on sank. He drowned, and carried the coin to the bottom of the bay.

The Fresno Tree

Captain Henry Malcolm was an American who lived for adventure. In 1865, he was in Mexico, fighting in a civil war under a general named Placido Vega.

When Vega became short of guns and ammunition, his supporters in Mexico gave him gold and jewels to buy what he needed. To do so, he sent a trusted friend to San Francisco with the treasure.

He also sent three of his officers. One was Captain Malcolm. The other two were a Mexican captain named Dávila and an English officer whose name has been forgotten. On the voyage north, the general's good friend died suddenly and mysteriously. The three officers suspected that enemy agents had poisoned him.

When they reached San Francisco, they decided to bury the treasure until they learned what General Vega wanted them to do. They divided it into six packages wrapped in buckskin, then rode on horseback into the hills near San Bruno and buried them in a grove of live oak trees.

An old Mexican shepherd named Diego Moreno was watching them as his sheep grazed nearby. That night, Moreno dug up the six packages and took them to his hut. When he opened one, he was astonished. Never before had he seen such riches. Inside were jewels, gold watches, and gold coins.

He quickly hid the packages under his bed. Day after day, he wondered what to do with them. Night after night, he slept with a pistol by his side to protect them. Finally he decided to return to Mexico, taking them with him. He bought a mule to ride and two burros to carry his things, and he headed south.

After many days, Diego Moreno reached the Cahuenga Pass, outside Los Angeles, near where the Hollywood Bowl is today. He decided to rest there for a few weeks before going on to Mexico and found an inn nearby where he stayed.

Not far from the inn, he came upon a solitary fresno tree, a tree known elsewhere as the wild ash. Around it he dug six holes, in which he buried the six packages of treasure. When he was ready to move on, he would come back for them.

But he became ill, and another Mexican, Don Jesús

Martínez, took him into his home and nursed him back to health. When Diego Moreno recovered, he said to Martínez, "I have a treasure I want to share with you for saving my life."

He told him how he had buried the treasure near the fresno tree. As he started to describe just where the tree was, he dropped dead. He was the second person who was involved with the treasure to die.

Martínez and his son Gumisindo searched for the fresno tree. When finally they found it, Martínez also collapsed and died. Now three were dead. The coincidence was so strange, Gumisindo fled in terror.

Meanwhile, General Vega had come to San Francisco to buy the guns he needed. Captain Malcolm, Captain Dávila, and the English officer went back to San Bruno to dig up the six packages they had buried. But the packages were gone.

Captain Dávila accused the English officer of stealing them. The Englishman hit him, and Dávila drew his knife. The Englishman drew his pistol. Before Captain Malcolm could stop them, they had killed one another. Now five were dead.

Twenty years passed. A shepherd grazing a flock of sheep in the Cahuenga Pass noticed his dog scratching at the ground near a fresno tree. He got a shovel and began digging. Soon he came to a package wrapped in buckskin. Inside were jewels, gold watches, and gold coins.

He told the man who ran the inn nearby what he had found, then gave him a few coins and pledged him to secrecy. With the rest he returned to his homeland in Spain. To protect the treasure, he carried it in a special garment that he wore under his regular clothes.

When his ship arrived, he climbed up on the railing to wave to his friends on the dock. But he lost his balance and fell into the water. The weight of the treasure pulled him under. He was the sixth to die.

Captain Malcolm, meanwhile, had gone to Tombstone, Arizona, to prospect for gold. He had filed a claim for a piece of land but got into an argument over it with another prospector. The man shot and killed him. He was the seventh to die.

By now, Martínez's son Gumisindo was a policeman in Los Angeles. He tried to find the fresno tree again, but this time he could not locate it. He decided that someone had cut the tree down. Then he met a newspaperman named Horace Bell.

Bell had been a friend of Captain Malcolm's and knew the story of the treasure up to the time when it had disappeared in San Bruno. He also knew about the shepherd who had found one of the six packages of treasure in the pass. The innkeeper there had told him about it.

Bell and Gumisindo joined forces to search for the five remaining packages. They would rent the land where Diego Moreno had buried them and plow it deeply enough to turn them up. But someone shot and killed Gumisindo. Now eight were dead. Bell gave up the search.

Some Wine to Celebrate

TWO MEN FOUND A TREASURE that would make them rich for the rest of their lives. While one guarded it, the other went to buy some food and wine to celebrate.

As he rode into town, he thought, "Why should I share these riches with him? I will poison the wine, and when he drinks it, all of the treasure will be mine."

While he was away, his friend sat against a tree, staring at the treasure. He thought, "Why should I share these riches with him? When he returns, I will kill him, and all of the treasure will be mine."

When the man returned from town, his partner shot him, then poured himself a glass of wine. As he sipped it, he thought, "What a pity I had to kill him." And he fell to the ground, dead.

10

HAUNTED TREASURE

People once believed that some buried treasures were haunted. Pirate treasure was said to be guarded by ghosts. And so were other treasures here and there.

Anyone who searched for a haunted treasure had to follow certain rules. Usually he had to search at night, and he had to remain silent. If he uttered even a sound, the treasure would disappear, or the ghost would drive him off. But there were also ghosts who had rules of their own.

Between the Giant Roots

HALFWAY UP THE HUDSON RIVER IN NEW YORK STATE, there is a grove of trees that are so big their branches overlap. Hardly any light ever reaches the ground. At the center of this grove is a tree that is even larger than the others.

One night an old woman who lived nearby read in her grandmother's diary that there was gold at the bottom of that giant tree. It was between two of its huge roots. But it was pirate gold, and nobody could get at it. Two of her friends swore the story was true.

The next night, she sent her two sons, Tom and Matt, to get the treasure. They loaded a pick, a shovel, a crowbar, and a lantern in their wagon, along with a potato sack in which to bring back whatever they found. Then they added a shotgun, just in case.

There was a full moon but in the darkness of those trees one would never have known it. With the hooting of owls, the swishing of bats, and the twisted shadows the lantern threw, it was a scary place.

Matt held the lantern, and Tom began digging between two of the giant roots. Soon there was a deep hole and next to it a big pile of dirt. When Tom got tired, Matt took over.

But as Tom climbed out of the hole, his eyes opened wide. A man dressed like an old-time seaman was standing in the shadows, watching them. When Matt saw the expression on Tom's face, he turned to see what his brother was staring at. He took one look and whispered, "Let's get out of here!" They dropped their tools, jumped into the wagon, and tore down the road for home.

When they went back for their things the next morning, the hole they had dug was gone, and so was the pile of dirt. Moss was growing there. It was as if the ground had never been touched, as if they had dreamed it all. But their tools were just where they had dropped them.

Under the Silk-Cotton Tree

A GHOST CAME TO A MAN IN A DREAM. It told him of a big iron box filled with gold coins that was buried under a silk-cotton tree way up the Supanaan River in Guyana, South America.

"But you must take only one handful," the ghost said.

The man decided not to search for the treasure. It was too far to go for just one handful of gold. But before he died, he told his son about the dream. His son also thought it was too far to go. But before *he* died, he told his son.

His son did not think it was too far to go. And he did not care what the ghost had said. If he found the gold, he would take it all, not just one handful. Then he would be rich. So he went, and later he told this story:

"I made the long, dangerous journey up the Supanaan River and found the silk-cotton tree. I dug around it and under it and into its roots—and there was the iron box, just as the ghost had said.

"The lid was stuck, but I got it loose and pushed it back. The box was filled to overflowing with gold coins. I plunged both hands in up to my wrists to take as much as I could as fast as I could. Then suddenly the lid slammed down!"

He stopped.

"What happened then?" someone asked.

He held out his arms. Both hands were gone.

In a Field Behind the Beach

YEARS AGO, YOUNG PETER HOSKINS and some of his shipmates came ashore on an isolated beach. In a field behind the beach, they dug a deep hole, and into it they lowered a chest of gold.

"Who will guard the treasure until we return?" the captain asked. Being new at this, Peter said that he would. The others promptly killed him. They threw his body on top of the treasure chest and filled in the hole.

As almost every pirate knew, it was the best way. Now Peter would not get bored and leave. And his ghost would faithfully guard the treasure, if necessary, for as long as Peter would have lived.

Then the pirates sailed away in search of more plunder. And Peter's ghost stood guard and waited for them to return. For twenty years he waited, but they did not come back. Each year he grew more and more restless. Yet he had to remain until somebody took the treasure or until his time was up.

Finally he thought of a way out. He would tell the next person he saw about the chest of gold. Then that person would quickly dig it up, and he would be free.

When at last a man came down that lonely beach, the ghost said, "If you would like a chest of gold, just follow me." But the man took one look at him and screamed and ran off. Each time the ghost offered the gold to someone, the same thing happened.

If he ever speaks to you, *don't* run! Follow him!

NOTES
SOURCES
BIBLIOGRAPHY

Notes

For the publications cited, see the Bibliography.

The Stories. Half the stories in this book are true. Others are legends that contain fact and fiction in varying amounts and cannot be verified. One is a folktale. The Sources indicate the type of story.

Gold and Silver. One reason these metals are so valuable is that they are so rare. They do not exist in most places, and where they do they are not easy to find. But there are other factors.

Gold and silver are both unusually beautiful. The color of gold has great depth and warmth and glows in an extraordinary way. Silver has a soft, lustrous quality. In its pure state it is almost white. In addition, both can be formed into almost any shape. Treasure hunters have found church bells, bullets, arrowheads, and whistles made from them, as well as chairs and a staircase made of gold.

Gold has another important quality. It is almost as dense as lead and, as a result, is virtually impossible to destroy. Even if it is under water for a thousand years, it will remain as it was the day it sank. Silver is softer and corrodes more readily.

Gold has always been the more valuable. When this was written, gold that had not yet been put to use was valued at over four hundred dollars an ounce; silver was worth five dollars an ounce.

In the Middle Ages, alchemists tried to create gold from other metals. They reduced a metal like copper to a molten state, then added some secret ingredient, but the best they could do was change the color. In modern times, nuclear physicists succeeded where the alchemists had failed. They turned platinum into gold by bombarding it with atomic particles from radium. But the gold was radioactive, and no treasure hunter would have been interested. See Dranof, Brynko.

Treasure Cities (The Search). Wherever men explored in the New World, they heard of mythical treasure cities like El Dorado and searched for them.

In Mexico, the Spaniard Francisco de Coronado set out in 1540 in search of the seven golden cities of Cibola. It was said that gold was as common in Cibola as stone, that each of the seven cities had a gate of gold; that people lived in palaces decorated with sapphires, emeralds, and other jewels.

Coronado took three hundred soldiers on horseback with him, along with a thousand Indians, herds of sheep and hogs for food, and six swivel guns of the latest design. He traveled northeast into what is now Arizona, then into the country of the Zuñi Indians in New Mexico. Finally he reached Cibola. Instead of palaces decorated with jewels, he found only pueblos carved in cliffs and huts built from mud.

Coronado then heard of the great riches of Quivera, a series of cities to the east where, it was said, people ate from dishes of gold. He and his men traveled on and on, another thousand miles in all, until finally they reached Quivera, a collection of wretched Indian villages in Kansas.

In 1595, the Englishman Sir Walter Raleigh traveled three hundred miles up the Orinoco River into the wilds of Guiana in search of a treasure city called Manoa. The Indians said it was guarded by men with eyes in their shoulders and mouths in their chests. He did not see such men on that journey, nor did he find Manoa. Twenty years later, when he was over sixty years old, he returned from England to hunt for it again, but once more it eluded him.

There were scores of such imaginary places: the golden city of Norembega on the coast of northern New England; the Seven Hills of the Aijados in Texas, where Indians were supposed to use gold arrowheads; the Peak of Gold and the Laguna del Oro in New Mexico; the palace of Cubanacán in Cuba; the Casa del Sol and the Golden Temple of Dabaiba in South America; and others. See Bandelier, pp. 9–30; Dobie, *Coronado,* pp. xvii–xxi; various encyclopedias.

Pieces of Eight and Doubloons (Chapter 3). The famous pieces of eight that treasure hunters sometimes find are silver coins that Spain used in the sixteenth and seventeenth centuries. One such coin was worth eight *reals*, which is why it was called a "piece of eight." The equally famous doubloons are gold coins the Spaniards also used.

Treasure Maps (Chapter 6). You are not likely to find in a book a treasure map that actually leads to treasure. People who have such maps guard them closely until they have found the treasure the map promises.

Treasure maps that have already been used are almost as hard to find. Often they continue to remain a secret, for their owners think there is more treasure to be found. Or they have so little detail that they mean something only to the person who drew them, and often he or she is dead. Or they have been destroyed or lost. In my search for real treasure maps, I did not find any that seemed worth including in this book.

I turned instead to the most famous of all treasure maps, the imaginary one in Robert Louis Stevenson's book *Treasure Island*, with its notes and directions that resembled in some ways those on the real map that George Brenner found in the story "12 Fathom NE" in Chapter 1.

There are two versions of how the map of Treasure Island came to be. Stevenson said he drew the map one rainy afternoon in Scotland for his stepson Lloyd Osborne, who was home from boarding school. Years later, Lloyd Osborne said *he* was the one who drew the map that rainy day and was coloring it when his stepfather came into the room.

". . . he leaned over my shoulder and was soon elaborating the map and naming it," Osborne wrote. "I shall never forget the thrill of Skeleton Island, Spy Glass Hill, nor the stirring climax of the three red crosses! And the greatest climax came when he wrote down the words 'Treasure Island' at the top right-hand corner."

In either case, Stevenson based his book on the map. The map so fascinated him that each day for fifteen days he wrote a chapter. Then that night Stevenson would read it to his wife and stepson and to his father who lived with them. When the story was sent to a publisher, the map was also sent, but was lost. Three years after the first map was created, Stevenson had to create a second one.

"It is one thing," he wrote, "to draw a map at random . . . set a scale of it in one corner . . . and write up a story to the measurements. It is quite another to have to examine a whole book . . . and with a pair of compasses painfully design a map to suit the data." Stevenson's father added the red *X*'s, the sailing directions, and the initials of the pirate, Captain Flint. See Stevenson, pp. x–xi, xxi–xxv, xxix.

The Beale Ciphers (Chapter 6). For a newsletter and other information on this subject, send $2 and a stamped, self-addressed business envelope to the Beale Cypher Association, P.O. Box 236, Warrington, PA 18976.

Cipher number 1, which is said to give the location of the treasure, is in Chapter 6. Cipher number 2, which has been solved, and cipher number 3, which has not, are on pages 118 and 119.

More Ways of Searching for Treasure (Chapter 7). Treasure hunters have used many methods in addition to those described in this chapter.

In the past, people depended on crystal balls to find treasure, and they also trusted dreams. If a person dreamed three times in succession of where a treasure lay, he took it as a clear sign of where to search.

A widespread folktale was based on this belief. It told of a man who dreamed three times that he would find a treasure if he went to a certain town and waited three days along a certain road. While he waited, a farmer asked him what he was doing there, and he told him about the treasure dreams.

The farmer then told of a similar dream he once had. He had dreamed that there was gold behind a house many miles away. When the farmer described the place, the man realized that he was talking about *his* house. "Of course, I paid no attention," the farmer said. "If I followed all my dreams, I would starve to death."

The man quickly returned home and dug in the spot the farmer had described. He came to an old box. In some versions of the tale, the box was filled with money. In others, it was empty. See Withers; Dobie, *Coronado*, pp. 305–6; Briggs, pp. 46–7.

In modern times, treasure hunters also have used remote-control television cameras to find treasure in the ocean. Aerial photography has found ballast piles of old treasure galleons and disclosed where buildings once stood that had served as landmarks for a buried treasure. In addition, scientists have experimented with a form of radar that used cosmic rays to search mountains and caves, but had not succeeded when this was written. See Marx, pp. 128–30.

One of the longest searches for a treasure took one hundred and forty years and failed. It involved the British frigate *Lutine*, which sank off the Netherlands in 1799 with over a million English pounds in gold and silver. The area was so exposed to rough seas, high winds, and shifting sands that salvage work was almost impossible.

At first, the treasure hunters used giant nippers, or tongs, that they operated from a search vessel and recovered several bars of gold and silver that had spilled on the ocean floor. It was the only real success they had. In later years, they tried a newly invented deep-sea-diving suit, but failed to find treasure. Then they used a steam dredge to remove the overburden of sand, and that did not succeed.

In 1910, they hoisted a huge steel tube into an upright position over the wreck. The tube was a hundred feet high, had a staircase inside, tackle for hoisting loads of treasure, and windows and a door at the bottom. It had no floor. The idea was to pump out any water inside, then use the tube as a base from which divers could reach the wreck. However, the engineers could not keep the water out.

A final attempt at the treasure was made in the 1930s, when one of the world's largest dredges was anchored over the wreck. It sucked up great amounts of sand and bits and pieces of the *Lutine*, but little treasure. See Paine, pp. 288–306; Nesmith, pp. 132–56.

Treasure and the Law (Chapter 7). Many governments claim a share of any sunken treasure found in their coastal waters. The state of Delaware, for example, claims 25 percent of the value of any treasure found in its waters. It also charges underwater treasure hunters a search fee of $1,500 and an additional $20,000 to lease a section of the ocean floor after they have located a potential source of treasure. See Robbins, "Shipwrecks."

CIPHER NUMBER 2: THE CONTENTS OF THE VAULT

115	73	24	818	37	52	49	17	31	62
657	22	7	15	140	47	29	107	79	84
56	238	10	26	822	5	195	308	85	52
159	136	59	210	36	9	46	316	543	122
106	95	53	58	2	42	7	35	122	53
31	82	77	250	195	56	96	118	71	140
287	28	353	37	994	65	147	818	24	3
8	12	47	43	59	818	45	316	101	41
78	154	994	122	138	190	16	77	49	102
57	72	34	73	85	35	371	59	195	81
92	190	106	273	60	394	629	270	219	106
388	287	63	3	6	190	122	43	233	400
106	290	314	47	48	81	96	26	115	92
157	190	110	77	85	196	46	10	113	140
353	48	120	106	2	616	61	420	822	29
125	14	20	37	105	28	248	16	158	7
35	19	301	125	110	496	287	98	117	520
62	51	219	37	113	140	818	138	549	8
44	287	388	117	18	79	344	34	20	59
520	557	107	612	219	37	66	154	41	20
50	6	584	122	154	248	110	61	52	33
30	5	38	8	14	84	57	549	216	115
71	29	85	63	43	131	29	138	47	73
238	549	52	53	79	118	51	44	63	195
12	238	112	3	49	79	353	105	56	371
566	210	515	125	360	133	143	101	15	284
549	252	14	204	140	344	26	822	138	115
48	73	34	204	316	616	63	219	7	52
150	44	52	16	40	37	157	818	37	121
12	95	10	15	35	12	131	62	115	102
818	49	53	135	138	30	31	62	67	41
85	63	10	106	818	138	8	113	20	32
33	37	353	287	140	47	85	50	37	49
47	64	6	7	71	33	4	43	47	63
1	27	609	207	229	15	190	246	85	94
520	2	270	20	39	7	33	44	22	40
7	10	3	822	106	44	496	229	353	210
199	31	10	38	140	297	61	612	320	302
676	287	2	44	33	32	520	557	10	6
250	566	246	53	37	52	83	47	320	38
33	818	7	44	30	31	250	10	15	35
106	159	113	31	102	406	229	549	320	29
66	33	101	818	138	301	316	353	320	219
37	52	28	549	320	33	8	48	107	50
822	7	2	113	73	16	125	11	110	67
102	818	33	59	81	157	38	43	590	138
19	85	400	38	43	77	14	27	8	47
138	63	140	44	35	22	176	106	250	314
216	2	10	7	994	4	20	25	44	48
7	26	46	110	229	818	190	34	112	147
44	110	121	125	96	41	51	50	140	56
47	152	549	63	818	28	42	250	138	591
98	653	32	107	140	112	26	85	138	549
50	20	125	371	38	36	10	52	118	136
102	420	150	112	71	14	20	7	24	18
12	818	37	67	110	62	33	21	95	219
520	102	822	30	83	84	305	629	15	2
10	8	219	106	353	105	106	60	242	72
8	50	204	184	112	125	549	65	106	818
190	96	110	16	73	33	818	150	409	400
50	154	285	96	106	316	270	204	101	822
400	8	44	37	52	40	240	34	204	38
16	46	47	85	24	44	15	64	73	138
818	85	78	110	33	420	515	53	37	38
22	31	10	110	106	101	140	15	38	3
5	44	7	98	287	135	150	96	33	84
125	818	190	96	520	118	459	370	653	466
106	41	107	612	219	275	30	150	105	49
53	287	250	207	134	7	53	12	47	85
63	138	110	21	112	140	495	496	515	14
73	85	584	994	150	199	16	42	5	4
25	42	8	16	822	125	159	32	204	612
818	81	95	405	41	609	136	14	20	28
26	353	302	246	8	131	159	140	84	440
42	16	822	40	67	101	102	193	138	204
51	63	240	549	122	8	10	63	140	47
48	140	288							

CIPHER NUMBER 3: WHO WAS TO GET THE TREASURE

317	8	92	73	112	89	67	318	28	96
107	41	631	78	146	397	118	98	114	246
348	116	74	88	12	65	32	14	81	19
76	121	216	85	33	66	15	108	68	77
43	24	122	96	117	36	211	301	15	44
11	46	89	18	136	68	317	28	90	82
304	71	43	221	198	176	310	319	81	99
264	380	56	37	319	2	44	53	28	44
75	98	102	37	85	107	117	64	88	136
48	151	99	175	89	315	326	78	96	214
218	311	43	89	51	90	75	128	96	33
28	103	84	65	26	41	246	84	270	98
116	32	59	74	66	69	240	15	8	121
20	77	89	31	11	106	81	191	224	328
18	75	52	82	117	201	39	23	217	27
21	84	35	54	109	128	49	77	88	1
81	217	64	55	83	116	251	269	311	96
54	32	120	18	132	102	219	211	84	150
219	275	312	64	10	106	87	75	47	21
29	37	81	44	18	126	115	132	160	181
203	76	81	299	314	337	351	96	11	28
97	318	238	106	24	93	3	19	17	26
60	73	88	14	126	138	234	286	297	321
365	264	19	22	84	56	107	98	123	111
214	136	7	33	45	40	13	28	46	42
107	196	227	344	198	203	247	116	19	8
212	230	31	6	328	65	48	52	59	41
122	33	117	11	18	25	71	36	45	83
76	89	92	31	65	70	83	96	27	33
44	50	61	24	112	136	149	176	180	194
143	171	205	296	87	12	44	51	89	98
34	41	208	173	66	9	35	16	95	8
113	175	90	56	203	19	177	183	206	157
200	218	260	291	305	618	951	320	18	124
78	65	19	32	124	48	53	57	84	96
207	244	66	82	119	71	11	86	77	213
54	82	316	245	303	86	97	106	212	18
37	15	81	89	16	7	81	39	96	14
43	216	118	29	55	109	136	172	213	64
8	227	304	611	221	364	819	375	128	296
11	18	53	76	10	15	23	19	71	84
120	134	66	73	89	96	230	48	77	26
101	127	936	218	439	178	171	61	226	313
215	102	18	167	262	114	218	66	59	48
27	19	13	82	48	162	119	34	127	139
34	128	129	74	63	120	11	54	61	73
92	180	66	75	101	124	265	89	96	126
274	896	917	434	461	235	890	312	413	328
381	96	105	217	66	118	22	77	64	42
12	7	55	24	83	67	97	109	121	135
181	203	219	228	256	21	34	77	319	374
382	675	684	717	864	203	4	18	92	16
63	82	22	46	55	69	74	112	135	186
175	119	213	416	312	343	264	119	186	218
343	417	845	951	124	209	49	617	856	924
936	72	19	29	11	35	42	40	66	85
94	112	65	82	115	119	236	244	186	172
112	85	6	56	38	44	85	72	32	47
73	96	124	217	314	319	221	644	817	821
934	922	416	975	10	22	18	46	137	181
101	39	86	103	116	138	164	212	218	296
815	380	412	460	495	675	820	952		

Captain Kidd and the Politicians (Chapter 8). The story of Captain Kidd's downfall has a side that is not well known. It involves politicians and businessmen whose selfish interests ensured that Kidd would hang.

When England's King William ordered an expedition against the pirates, Governor Bellomont of New York saw a chance to make money. He and some partners decided to buy the ship that was needed. Under their agreement with the King, they would keep whatever booty was captured.

Bellomont's partners were some of the most powerful men in the British government, including the First Lord of the Admiralty, the Lord Chancellor, and the secretaries of state.

When Kidd agreed to lead the expedition, he also was made a partner. But when he captured the Great Mogul's ships and was accused of piracy, it caused trouble for the other partners. Parliament criticized them for their role in the affair. Fearful that Kidd would hurt their reputations even more, they wanted to see him hanged and worked for his conviction. The British East India Company, which did business with the Great Mogul, also wanted to see Kidd hanged. They wished to remain on good terms with this powerful ruler and thought Kidd's execution would help them to do so.

The government did everything it could to make certain that Kidd would be found guilty. As the story in Chapter 8 explains, Kidd's defense was based on two "French passes" he had found on the Mogul's ships. He said these proved he had taken the vessels as prizes of war, not as an act of piracy. Kidd had given Bellomont the passes as evidence, and Bellomont had promised to send them to England for the trial. The government said the passes did not exist, and Kidd was hung.

Two hundred years later, a writer named Ralph Paine found the passes in the Public Records Office in London. Bellomont *had* sent them. The government had lied. See Dow and Edmonds, pp. 73–85; Paine, pp. 103–5.

Kidd and the Song Writers. On the day in 1701 on which Captain Kidd was hanged, copies of a new ballad, "Captain Kidd's Farewell to the Sea, or the Famous Pirate's Lament," were sold to the huge crowd that had come to watch. It was one of a half-dozen songs that helped to spread the legend of Captain Kidd as a bloodthirsty pirate.

The ballad soon moved to the American colonies, where it was called "The Dying Words of Captain Robert Kidd," not William Kidd, and its lyrics changed somewhat. It was one of the first American ballads and was enormously popular. Verses from both versions are quoted in Chapter 8.

Kidd and the Storytellers. Over the years, a legend developed in which Captain Kidd became a supernatural figure who traveled in a phantom ship and used ghosts to guard his treasure. Several famous writers referred to this legend and his true experiences in their stories.

Edgar Allan Poe mentioned Kidd in "The Gold-Bug" (Chapter 6). Washington Irving used the legend of a supernatural pirate in his story "Wolfert Webber, or Golden Dreams" (Chapter 7). In "Wolfert Webber," Irving also created a buccaneer who said he was a former comrade of Kidd's. Robert Louis Stevenson used this pirate as a model for his pirate figures in *Treasure Island.* James Fenimore Cooper also referred to Kidd in several of his novels, including *The Deerslayer.* See Bonner, "The Flying Dutchman."

Sources

The source of each item is given. Publications are cited in the Bibliography.

He dreamed (epigraph). Irving, p. 240. Adapted for clarity.
The Search (Introduction). Bandelier, pp. 9–30; Paine, pp. 335–60; Dobie,
    Coronado, pp. xvii–xxii.

1. A Treasure Found

12 Fathom NE. Retold from Snow, pp. 167–9. A true story.

2. A Treasure Lost

Gold Lake. A largely true story retold from Ritchie, pp. 3–12; Bell,
    Reminiscences, pp. 463–5.
The Orange Trees. A legend adapted from Gilpatrick, pp. 52–64.
A Shiny Black Wall. An apparently true story from Hand, pp. 39–41,
    reported by James Nosser, Johannesburg, Cal., early 1940s.
    Adapted.

3. Pirate Ships and Spanish Galleons

The Whydah. A mixture of fact and fiction. Based on accounts in Dow
    and Edmonds, pp. 116–31; Reynard, pp. 214–23, citing Cape Cod
    legends and research by Michael Fitzgerald; Digges, pp. 152–4;
    Dorson, p. 187; "Coins from the Sea"; Wald.
The Atocha. A true story. Based on references in Lyon, "The Trouble
    with Treasure," "Treasure from the Ghost Galleon"; Daley; Dra-
    nov; "Divers Find Huge Trove of Silver"; "Florida Divers Retrieve
    Tons of Silver Bars"; Nordheimer.

4. The Pit and the Cave

The Bank on Oak Island. A true story. Based on "The Original Swiss Bank";

"Pirate Loot Still Sought in Canada"; references in Nesmith, pp. 116–31, citing Driscoll, Snow, various newspaper, magazine accounts; Creighton, *Bluenose Ghosts*, pp. 57–9.

Love, Death, and Gold. A legend retold from accounts in Granger, pp. 99–131.

5. THERE IT IS!

Five Fruit Jars. A true story based on articles in the *Des Moines* (Iowa) *Register.* See "Five Fruit Jars."

6. CODES, MAPS, AND SIGNS

Introduction. References to the story "The Gold Bug," Poe, pp. 449–476. References to *Treasure Island,* Stevenson, various.

Forty-five Pinholes. A true story from Snow, pp. 242–72. Adapted.

Three Ciphers. An apparent legend, retold from the *Beale Cypher Association Newsletter;* Burchard.

The Arrows and the Ring. An apparently true story. Dobie, *Coronado's Children,* pp. 298–302. Adapted. The symbols for "You are on the right trail" are from various sources.

A Golden Rabbit. A true story. Based on an account in *The Sunday Times,* London, March 14, 1982, as reported in Borders; Goodman; "Hare of the Dogged"; Williams.

7. THE NEEDLE IN A HAYSTACK

Doctor Knipperhausen and His Divining Rod. Retold from the Washington Irving story "Wolfert Webber, or Golden Dreams," Irving, pp. 449–76; "Divining Rods"; Hand, pp. 34–6.

Captain Phips and His Fantastic Good Luck. A largely true story based on accounts in Paine, pp. 128–58; Karraker, pp. 50–6; Mather, pp. 170–2.

Doctor Halley and His Diving Bell. Ronan, pp. 101–5; Halley, pp. 144–5, 150–6, 224–5; Karraker, pp. 82–3.

Captain Dickinson and His Giant Derrick. A true story based on an account by Dickinson as described in Paine, pp. 309–34.

Simon Lake's Baby Submarine. Manchester; "Midget Submarine to Seek Riches."

Echoes and Beeps. Robbins, "18th Century Wreck"; "Shipwrecks"; Blair; Marx, pp. 124–30; Dranov; Wagner.

8. The Curious Treasure of Captain Kidd

A mixture of fact and fiction. Based on accounts in Dow and Edmonds, pp. 73–85; Paine, pp. 26–128. The ballad stanzas are from Bonner, "The Ballad of Captain Kidd." For clarity, two changes were made in the first stanza: the spelling "Kid" was changed to "Kidd"; the word "still" was omitted.

9. No Good Came of It

The Message. Probably a legend. Adapted from "The Power of a Curse," *Rockland* (Maine) *Courier-Gazette,* March 22, 1938, as quoted in Dorson, pp. 186–7.

The Fresno Tree. A true story. Adapted from Bell, *On the Old West Coast,* pp. 60–71.

Some Wine to Celebrate. A widespread folktale. This variant is retold from Geoffrey Chaucer's "The Pardoner's Tale" in *The Canterbury Tales.* For an Ozark Mountains version, see Randolph, pp. 77–9.

10. Haunted Treasure

Between the Giant Roots. Retold from a legend reported in Jones, pp. 100–2.

Under the Silk-Cotton Tree. A retelling of a South American legend based on an account in Leach, pp. 41–2. Mrs. Leach collected this story from Arthur Goodland of Georgetown, Guyana, as it was told to him by Ray Wilkins. The Supanaan River is in central Guyana. The seeds of the silk-cotton tree are contained in a silky floss for which the tree is named.

In a Field Behind a Beach. This retelling of a legend known in Bonavista, Newfoundland, is based on an account in Patterson, p. 288.

Bibliography

BOOKS

Bailey, Philip. *Golden Mirages*. New York: The Macmillan Company, 1940. Reprint edition: Acoma Books, Ramona, Cal., 1971.

Bandelier, Adolph F. A. *The Gilded Man*. New York: D. Appleton and Company, 1893. Reprint edition: Rio Grande Press, Chicago, 1962.

Bell, Horace. *On the Old West Coast, Being Further Reminiscences of a Ranger*, ed. Lanier Bartlett. New York: William Morrow and Company, 1930.

———. *Reminiscences of a Ranger*. Santa Barbara, Cal.: W. Hebberd, 1927.

Briggs, Katharine M. *A Dictionary of British Folktales*. 4 vols. Bloomington: Indiana University Press, 1967.

Creighton, Helen. *Bluenose Ghosts*. Toronto: The Ryerson Press, 1957.

———. *Bluenose Magic*. Toronto: The Ryerson Press, 1968.

Daley, Robert. *Treasure*. New York: Random House, 1977.

Dickinson, Thomas. *"A Narrative of the Operations for the Recovery of the Public Stores and Treasure sunk in H.M.S. Thetis at Cape Frio on the coast of Brazil, on the Fifth December, 1836, to which is prefixed a Concise Account of the Loss of that Ship."* London: privately printed, 1836.

Digges, Jeremiah, pseudonym of Josef Berger. *Cape Cod Pilot*. Federal Writers' Project for the State of Massachusetts. Provincetown: Modern Pilgrim Press, 1937.

Dobie, J. Frank. *Apache Gold and Yaqui Silver*. Boston: Little, Brown and Company, 1939.

———. *Coronado's Children: Tales of Lost Mines and Buried Treasure of the Southwest*. Dallas: Southwest Press, 1930. Reprint edition: University of Texas Press, Austin, 1978.

Dorson, Richard. *Jonathan Draws the Long Bow*. Cambridge, Mass.: Harvard University Press, 1946.

Dow, George F., and John H. Edmonds. *The Pirates of the New England Coast*. Salem, Mass: Marine Research Society, 1923.

Gilpatrick, Wallace. *The Man Who Likes Mexico*. New York: The Century Co., 1911.

Granger, Byrd, *A Motif Index for Lost Mines and Treasures.* Tucson: University of Arizona Press, 1977.

Halley, Edmond. *Correspondence and Papers of Edmond Halley,* ed. Eugene F. MacPike. London: Oxford University Press, 1932. Reprint edition: Taylor and Francis, London, 1937.

Irving, Washington. *Tales of a Traveller,* vol. 2. New York: G. P. Putnam's Sons, 1897.

Jones, Louis C. *Things That Go Bump in the Night.* New York: Hill and Wang, 1959.

Karraker, Cyrus H. *The Hispaniola Treasure.* Philadelphia: University of Pennsylvania Press, 1934.

Leach, Maria. *The Thing at the Foot of the Bed.* New York: The Viking Press, 1974.

Marx, Robert F. *Buried Treasure of the United States.* New York: David McKay Company, 1978.

Mather, Cotton. *Magnalia Christi, or the Ecclesiastical History of New England.* Hartford, Conn.: Silas Andrus & Son, 1855.

Nesmith, Robert I. *Dig for Pirate Treasure.* New York: Devin-Adair Company, 1958.

Paine, Ralph D. *The Book of Buried Treasure.* New York: The Macmillan Company, 1922.

Poe, Edgar Allan. *The Complete Poems and Stories of Edgar Allan Poe,* vol. 1. New York: Alfred A. Knopf, 1946.

Randolph, Vance. *Sticks in the Knapsack and Other Ozark Tales.* New York: Columbia University Press, 1958.

Reynard, Elizabeth. *The Narrow Land: Folk Chronicles of Old Cape Cod.* 2d ed. Boston: Houghton Mifflin, 1968.

Ritchie, William Welles. *The Hell-Roarin' Forty-Niners.* New York: J. H. Sears & Company, 1928.

Ronan, Colin A. *Edmond Halley: Genius in Eclipse.* Garden City, N.Y.: Doubleday & Co., 1969.

Skinner, Charles M. *Myths and Legends of Our Own Land,* vol. 2. Philadelphia: J. B. Lippincott Company, 1896.

Snow, Edward Rowe. *True Tales of Buried Treasure.* New York: Dodd, Mead & Company, 1951.

Stevenson, Robert Louis. *The Works of Robert Louis Stevenson,* Vailina edition, vol. 5. New York: Charles Scribner's Sons, 1922.

Watson, Harold F. *Coasts of Treasure Island.* San Antonio, Texas: The Naylor Company, 1969.

Williams, Kit. *Masquerade.* New York: Schocken Books, 1980.

ARTICLES

Altrocchi, Julia C. "Folklore from the Old California Trail." *California Folklore Quarterly* 3 (1944): 1–8.

Beale Cypher Association Newsletter. Special edition, 1984.

Blair, William G. "In the East River, a Gold Frigate and High Hopes." *New York Times,* Sept. 26, 1985, p. 1.

Bonner, William H. "The Ballad of Captain Kidd." *American Literature* 15 (1944): 362–380.

———. "The Flying Dutchman of the Western World." *Journal of American Folklore* 59 (1946): 282–8.

——— "Hudson River Legends of Captain Kidd." *New York Folklore Quarterly* 2 (1946): 40–51.

Borders, William. "The British Treasure Hunt for the Jeweled Rabbit Is Over." *New York Times,* March 15, 1982, p. 1, summarizing an account in *The Sunday Times,* London, England, March 14, 1982.

Brynko, Barbara. "Gold Lust." *Science Digest,* Dec. 1982, p. 62.

Burchard, Hank. "Legendary Treasure Quests." *Washington Post,* Oct. 5, 1984, "Weekend" section, pp. 5–7.

"Coins from the Sea Might Solve a Pirate Mystery." *New York Times,* Jan. 8, 1985, p. 10.

"Divers Find Huge Trove of Silver in Lost Galleon." *New York Times,* July 21, 1979, p. 16.

"Divining Rods." *Columbia Encyclopedia,* 3d ed. New York: Columbia University Press, 1963.

Dranov, Paula. "Hi-Tech Treasure Hunt." *Science Digest,* Dec. 1982, pp. 61–5.

Fauset, Arthur H. "Folklore from Nova Scotia." *Memoirs of the American Folklore Society* 34 (1931): pp. 140–76.

"Five Fruit Jars." Articles in the *Des Moines* (Iowa) *Register:* "Bayard Boys Find Treasure," June 2, 1965; "$11,500 Found by Boys—$478 Each," Dec. 18, 1968; "Treasure Days Over," Nov. 2, 1969; "Adult Greed Dulls Boys' Treasure," Nov. 2, 1980.

"Florida Divers Retrieve Tons of Silver Bars." *New York Times,* July 22, 1985, p. 8.

"Gold Diggers of 1973." *Newsweek,* Sept. 3, 1973, pp. 56–7.

Goodman, Susan. "The Legend of the Golden Hare." *New York Times Magazine,* Nov. 15, 1981, p. 64.

Hand, Wayland D. "California Miners' Folklore: Above Ground," *California Folklore Quarterly* 1 (1942): 24–46, 34–6.

"Hare of the Dogged." *Time,* March 29, 1982, p. 44.

"Hidden Treasure?" *Newsweek,* Nov. 8, 1971, pp. 71–2.

Klinck, Richard E. "Desert Treasure." *Western Folklore* 12 (1953): 25–9.

Lyon, Eugene. "The Trouble with Treasure." *National Geographic,* June 1976, pp. 787–809.

———. "Treasure from the Ghost Galleon." *National Geographic,* Feb. 1982, pp. 231–43.

Manchester, Harland. "Simon Lake, Submarine Genius." *Scientific American,* March 1943, pp. 120–3.

"Midget Submarine to Seek Riches on Sea's Floor." *Popular Science Monthly,* March 1933, pp. 22–3.

Nordheimer, Jon. "Archaeologists' Eyes Glittering Over Treasure." *New York Times,* July 24, 1985, p. 1.

"The Original Swiss Bank." *Forbes,* Nov. 15, 1974, p. 84.

Patterson, George. "Notes on the Folk-Lore of Newfoundland." *Journal of American Folklore* 8 (1895): 285–90.

"Pirate Loot Still Sought in Canada." *New York Times,* March 2, 1975, p. 6.

Robbins, William. "18th Century Wreck Yields Gold Ring and Trove of Coins." *New York Times,* Sept. 18, 1984, p. 1.

———. "Shipwrecks Make Some Go Diving for Dollars." *New York Times,* Oct. 7, 1984, IV, p. 10.

Tolman, Ruth B. "Treasure Tales from the Caballos." *Western Folklore* 20 (1961): 153–74.

Wagner, Kip. "Drowned Galleons Yield Spanish Gold." *National Geographic,* Jan. 1985, pp. 1–37.

Wald, Matthew. "Bell Confirms That Salvors Found Pirate Ship of Legend." *New York Times,* Nov. 1, 1985, p. 1.

Withers, Carl. "The Treasure at Home," *Journal of American Folklore* 78 (1965): 68–9.